the Prairie Thief

Melissa Wiley

With illustrations by Erwin Madrid

Margaret K. McElderry Books
New York   London   Toronto   Sydney   New Delhi

MARGARET K. McELDERRY BOOKS

An imprint of Simon & Schuster Children's Publishing Division

1230 Avenue of the Americas, New York, New York 10020

This book is a work of fiction. Any references to historical events, real people, or real places are used fictitiously. Other names, characters, places, and events are products of the author's imagination, and any resemblance to actual events or places or persons, living or dead, is entirely coincidental.

Text copyright © 2012 by Melissa Anne Peterson

Illustrations copyright © 2012 by Erwin Madrid

All rights reserved, including the right of reproduction in whole or in part in any form.

MARGARET K. MCELDERRY BOOKS is a trademark of Simon & Schuster, Inc.

For information about special discounts for bulk purchases, please contact Simon & Schuster Special Sales at 1-866-506-1949 or business@simonandschuster.com.

The Simon & Schuster Speakers Bureau can bring authors to your live event. For more information or to book an event, contact the Simon & Schuster Speakers Bureau at 1-866-248-3049 or visit our website at www.simonspeakers.com.

Also available in a Margaret K. McElderry Books hardcover edition

Book design by Sonia Chaghatzbanian

The text for this book is set in Adobe Caslon Pro.

The illustrations for this book are rendered in Photoshop.

Manufactured in the United States of America

0820 OFF

First Margaret K. McElderry Books paperback edition August 2013

8 10 9 7

The Library of Congress has cataloged the hardcover edition as follows:

Wiley, Melissa.

The prairie thief / Melissa Wiley ; with illustrations by Erwin Madrid.

p. cm.

Summary: In late nineteenth-century Colorado, Louisa's father is erroneously arrested for thievery and, while under the charge of the awful Smirch family, Louisa and a magical friend must find a way to prove his innocence.

ISBN 978-1-4424-4056-2 (hardcover)

ISBN 978-1-4424-4058-6 (eBook)

[1. Magic—Fiction. 2. Prairies—Fiction.] I. Madrid, Erwin, ill. II. Title.

PZ7.W64814Pr 2012

[Fic]—dc23

2011047642

ISBN 978-1-4424-4057-9 (pbk)

*Dedicated to
the Plains Conservation Center
in Aurora, Colorado,
where the pronghorn roam*

Contents

August 9, 1882

Dear Judge Callahan—

I sorely hate to ask this of you, seeing as we weren't expecting you back in Fletcher until next month. If it ain't too great an inconvenience, I'd be obliged if you'd catch the next stage back to town. I've got just about the last person on earth you'd expect sitting in my jail right this minute. Jack Brody's been accused of thievery. Got to say, Judge, it don't look good for him. I hope you'll come back and get it sorted for us.

—Chester Morgan, County Sheriff

CHAPTER ONE
It Ain't Right

THE SMIRCHES TOOK LOUISA IN WHEN HER PA WENT to jail, but they weren't happy about it.

"Another mouth to feed," griped Mrs. Smirch. Her cold eyes looked Louisa up and down. "And she's too puny to be any help around this place. I can't fathom what got into your head, Malcolm."

Mr. Smirch shrugged. His lips were pressed into a thin line. He had the same grim look on his face Louisa's pa always had when it was time to kill a pig—the look of someone who can't get out of doing a thing he hates to do.

"Don't see as we had much choice in the matter, Matilda," he said. "Sheriff only had the one horse."

Louisa blinked hard, trying to stop picturing Pa riding away on that horse, hatless, his red hair blowing back, sitting in front of the sheriff with his hands tied, looking over his shoulder at her until the sheriff cuffed him on the arm and made him face front. Before he turned away, Pa had winked at her; that was the worst part. She had almost cried then. But Mr. Smirch had been standing beside her, and she would sooner have died than shed a tear in front of the man who had called the law upon her father.

Now here she was in that man's own house, being scowled at by his wife, a wispy-haired woman with sharp eyes and a greasy apron. The little Smirch boys, Winthrop and Charlie, stood behind their mother, making faces at Louisa when their pa wasn't looking. Near the table, a young girl with long straggly braids stood working butter in a churn that was almost as big as she was. She was staring at Louisa, smiling a little as she thumped the wooden dash up and down, up and down. Louisa remembered Mr. Smirch telling her pa—was it really only the day before yesterday?—that his nine-year-old niece had arrived on the train from Topeka a week or two earlier. That had been right before Winthrop came charging down the hill from the old dugout, jabbering about Mrs. Smirch's missing clock and Mr. Smirch's lost hatchet. Louisa could still picture the way the friendly look on Mr. Smirch's face had gone sharp and wary, his eyes narrowing at Pa.

"I never heard of such nonsense," muttered Mrs. Smirch, hands on her hips. "Man robs us blind, and the sheriff expects us to look after his young'un? Trained to thieve herself, I shouldn't wonder. You best not try any tricks here, girl, you hear me? There's room in that there jail cell for you too, and don't you forget it."

Louisa breathed hard, too angry to speak. *My pa's no thief,* she wanted to holler, but she couldn't say one word. All she could do was stand there stone-faced, looking at Mrs. Smirch.

"Don't you glare at me, child. You ought to be grateful we was willin' to take you in." Mrs. Smirch whipped around to stir something in a pot on the iron stove, clattering her tin ladle angrily against the sides. Winthrop Smirch, the six-year-old, snickered and stuck out his tongue at Louisa. *And to think I gave you fresh biscuits the other day,* Louisa thought furiously. She remembered how that visit had ended and had to swallow hard again. If Winthrop and Charlie Smirch hadn't poked their noses where they didn't belong, she might not be standing in this miserable kitchen right now.

Mrs. Smirch resumed berating her husband.

"Sheriff ought to come back for the child himself, if you ask me. It ain't right, our havin' to keep her."

"It's thirteen miles each way, Matilda," said Mr. Smirch wearily. "Man's got a job to do in town. Can't be traipsin' back and forth across the prairie."

"Then he ought to send someone else to fetch her," snapped Mrs. Smirch.

"She can ride in the wagon when I take the wheat in," said Mr. Smirch. "We ain't got to keep her all that long."

His wife snorted. "It'll be weeks before you get that crop in. And her eatin' us out of house and home all that time."

Louisa opened her mouth to protest, but she was stopped short by a giggle from the girl at the butter churn. Mrs. Smirch whirled around, clutching her ladle.

"Jessamine! What are you snickerin' about, girl?" she demanded.

"Sorry, ma'am," said the little girl. "It's just . . . I don't guess Louisa could eat us out of house and home, seeing as she's so *puny* and all."

"Don't you dare sass me, girl!" Mrs. Smirch brought the tin ladle down—*smack*—on top of the girl's head. Louisa gasped. The little girl's face turned red, and her lips pinched together. She went back to churning, thumping the dash over and over with all her might.

Louisa felt sick to her stomach. She had never seen a grown-up hit a child before. But then, living so far from town, Louisa had hardly ever been around any other families. After the Smirches, the next nearest neighbors were some six miles away.

Maybe, thought Louisa, that was how people in other families treated each other. A horrible ache rose in her throat.

Oh, Pa, she thought. *How could you let this happen?*

CHAPTER TWO
Not a Critter

NONE OF IT SEEMED REAL—NOT PA'S ARREST, NOR having to stay with the very people who'd had him arrested, nor finding herself, that night, squeezed onto a prickly straw tick alongside three other children. Louisa lay in the stuffy darkness trying not to think of Pa, far away in town, sleeping behind bars in the county jail. She'd never been this far away from him her whole life; he'd always taken her with him on trips to town, letting her pick some ribbon candy and licorice whips out of the big glass jars in the Fletcher general store. She hated the feel of the lump in her throat that wouldn't go away.

It was hard to sleep, crammed between the rough wall and Jessamine, with Winthrop and Charlie breathing heavily on Jessamine's other side. Straw poked Louisa through the mattress cover. When she rolled over, the straw shifted inside the canvas so that she was lying in a flat trough on the hard plank floor. Around her the air hung heavy with heat and shadows. She ached for her own bed in her nice, neat, whitewashed room at home.

It was still dark when Mrs. Smirch commenced rapping on the wall with something—probably that battered ladle of which she seemed so fond—to wake the girls and Mr. Smirch. Louisa couldn't see the room around her as she fumbled into her dress and knit stockings. When she bumped into a chair, Mrs. Smirch fussed at her for making noise.

"You'll wake the little'uns," she hissed, as if she hadn't just been hammering on the wall with a large tin spoon.

Louisa ate a breakfast of thick, lumpy, unsalted cornmeal mush across the table from a silent, brooding Mr. Smirch, while Mrs. Smirch huffed around the small kitchen with her creased skirts swishing. Jessamine sat beside Louisa, eating mechanically, with her eyes on Mrs. Smirch. When she glanced at Louisa, an eager little smile darted across her face.

Poor thing, thought Louisa. *It's probably awful for her here too.* She couldn't imagine having Mrs. Smirch for kin.

Crack! The ever-present ladle came down suddenly on Louisa's head. Louisa yelped, her hand flying to her head. The pain brought tears to her eyes.

"Eat up, girl!" snarled Mrs. Smirch. "What's the matter with you?"

"Now, Matilda," faltered Mr. Smirch.

Mrs. Smirch whipped around, turning her buzzard's glare on her husband. "Don't you 'now Matilda' me, Malcolm Smirch. If you had the sense God gave a gopher, we'd be chargin' this child board."

Mr. Smirch abruptly pushed back his chair and stood up. For a moment Louisa thought he was going to light into Mrs. Smirch, but all he said was "Got my chores to do," and clomped out the door in his heavy boots.

Mrs. Smirch whirled back to Louisa, brandishing her ladle ominously. "You best not let that good food go to waste, you hear me?"

"Good" is a bit of a stretch, Louisa thought, but she dutifully choked down another spoonful of the unsavory paste, resisting the urge to rub her still-tingling scalp.

Mrs. Smirch eyed her a moment, then turned and strode across the room to the lean-to.

The moment her aunt was out of earshot, Jessamine leaned close to Louisa.

"Don't mind Aunt Mattie. She's always cross in the mornings." She seemed to consider a moment. "Well, and also the afternoons. Anyway, listen: I know a secret!" Her head was so close to Louisa, they were practically cheek to cheek. "There's something living in our hazel grove," Jessamine whispered. "Something *peculiar*. Don't tell anyone, 'specially not the boys."

Louisa didn't see what was so secret about something living in the hazel grove. Probably *lots* of things lived in the hazel grove: snakes and birds and mice and maybe even a raccoon or two. But tiny Jessamine with her spiky braids and quick smile was the only person in the Smirch home who'd been nice to her, and Louisa didn't want to hurt her feelings. She nodded, promising not to tell.

"What kind of critter is it?" she asked, playing along.

Jessamine shook her head, glancing toward the lean-to.

"Ain't a critter," she said. "It's about the size of a woodchuck, but it wears a hat."

Louisa blinked. "A hat?"

"Yup, a funny brown one. It's pointy."

Mrs. Smirch came clattering back into the kitchen, a wooden pail in each hand. Jessamine stared a message at Louisa with imploring eyes.

Don't tell.

"Ain't you girls done yet? Hurry up! You got to fetch the water so's I can get them boys dressed."

Louisa didn't see what the one had to do with the other, but she didn't mind being sent for water. That was one of her jobs at home, too. She always liked to go out on cool summer mornings like this one, when the meadowlarks were singing love songs to the sky and the little blue-striped lizards were just coming out to sun themselves on the rocks. Today she was doubly glad to get outside—anything to get away from silent, glowering Mr. Smirch and his irritable wife. She carried her breakfast plate to the dishpan beside the iron stove and, taking up one of the water pails, followed Jessamine through the lean-to and out the door.

The sun was just rising above the undulating eastern plain, spilling gold onto the low-drifting clouds. As soon as the girls were clear of the house, Jessamine began to chatter, picking up right where she'd left off at the table.

"It wore a hat, Louisa, honest it did. Like the dunce cap on the picture of the bad boy in my ma's old lesson book."

Louisa stared at Jessamine, unsure what to make of her. She looked so bright and earnest; she didn't seem like the type to tell tales. Then again, maybe she needed tales to cheer herself up. Louisa had heard Mr. Smirch tell Pa all about how Jessamine's family had died of the cholera. All of them—her mother and father and big brother. It was the worst thing Louisa could imagine: losing Pa and having to come live with Mrs. Smirch not just for a while, but forever.

"Poor mite," Pa had said to Mr. Smirch. "It's a mercy she has you folks to come to. Be nice for your wife to have her company too, I bet. There's nothin' beats havin' a little girl around to talk your ear off and keep you lively." He'd shot a wink at Louisa, who'd been scattering scraps in the barnyard for the chickens. That time, Louisa had winked back. It was their special signal, their secret *I-love-you*.

Now, walking alongside Jessamine to the Smirches' spring, which seemed to be a good piece from the house, Louisa had to blink hard to keep the tears back. She missed Pa so much. Mr. Smirch had been nice the other morning, not sullen and glowering at all. Louisa didn't see how things could change so fast—how suddenly your friendly neighbor was calling your pa a liar and a thief and accusing him of stealing all sorts of valuables right out from under his nose.

It isn't true, she thought fiercely. *I don't care what they found in the dugout. It isn't true. My pa's no thief.*

"What do you suppose it is, Louisa?" Jessamine was asking. Louisa wrenched her mind away from thoughts of Pa and tried to pay attention to whatever this tall tale was that Jessamine was going on about. The younger girl was staring at her with eager eyes. Her faded gingham dress was too small, so that her wrists stuck out of the sleeves.

"I . . . I don't know," Louisa faltered. "I never heard of a critter that wears a pointy hat."

"That's why I say it ain't no critter," said Jessamine. "I don't know what it is. I only saw it from the back. It went down a hole by that big old boulder in the hazel grove. It was carrying a sack, like a flour sack, with bulges. It heard me squeak—'cause I was so surprised, you know—and it looked back over its shoulder and popped down that hole, quick as a jackrabbit. I only saw it for a second." She was talking rapidly, swinging her pail with excitement. "It wore some kind of little old patched-up coat and, Louisa, I could've sworn it had a *beard*."

Despite herself, Louisa laughed. A pointy hat and a beard? Maybe Jessamine was spinning tales to amuse herself and was little enough that she half believed them. Louisa didn't blame her. A couple of weeks in a house with Mrs. Smirch, and *anyone* would need some good stories to take her mind off her misery.

She decided it wouldn't do any harm to play along with the little girl's game.

"What color was the beard?" she asked.

Jessamine broke into a radiant smile. "Oh, Louisa! You believe me!" She shifted her pail to the other side and took Louisa's hand in hers. "I'm real sorry your pa's in trouble, but I'm glad you're staying with us for a while. Later I'll take you to the grove and show you where the hole is. Maybe we'll even see him again."

"Maybe," said Louisa. If an honest man like her pa could be carted off to jail in the blink of an eye, then most anything could happen.

CHAPTER THREE

As Plain as Pie

JUDGE CORNELIUS P. CALLAHAN SPEARED A POTATO with his fork, wishing he could pin down truth as easily as a spud. His bristly brows drew together into a frown as he chewed. His cook-and-housekeeper, Mrs. Mack, was offended, and she let him know it in no uncertain terms. Her exasperated *humph* roused him, bringing his thoughts back to her excellent herb gravy.

"Begging your pardon, ma'am," he said, for Judge Callahan prided himself on his good manners. "My mind, it runs away with me." He forked another chunk of potato and swirled it in the rich brown gravy. "Ah, me, 'tis good to be home, and early to boot. I do miss your fine cooking when I'm on the circuit."

Mrs. Mack sniffed, mollified, and stalked off to the kitchen, where there was a pie waiting to be cut. Judge Callahan smiled. Mrs. Mack was a touchy sort, fiercely proud and sharp of tongue. But there wasn't a public kitchen in the county that could beat her cooking—and that, the judge asserted to himself, was fact, not speculation. As a traveling circuit judge, he'd had occasion to eat at every boardinghouse and restaurant in a hundred-mile radius. Not one could boast a meal half so savory as Mrs. Mack's cooking. It was almost uncanny, thought the judge, the way that female put a meal together.

But as he scraped up the last bits of gravy from his dish—he'd have licked it clean, were it not a gross breach of manners—his mind returned to the troubling situation that had met him on his hasty return to Fletcher after he'd received Sheriff Morgan's letter. Jack Brody, a man Judge Callahan would have testified was one of the most solid and upstanding citizens in the county, was locked up in the town jail on suspicion of theft.

Not just petty theft, either—a low-down, sneaky, systematic kind of thievery the like of which Judge Callahan had never seen in all his years on the bench. It appeared that Jack Brody had been snatching goods from right under the nose of his closest neighbor and purported friend. The robberies must have been going on for months—if the facts were indeed as Sheriff Morgan had laid out for the judge, and though Judge Callahan held it as a matter of honor never to jump to a verdict before a fair trial, he had to admit that things looked black for Jack Brody. Stolen valuables found stashed in Brody's old dugout; no other neighbors within miles. No reports of strangers in the area, either.

"I'd never have believed it of him," said Judge Callahan, shaking his head, as Mrs. Mack replaced his stew plate with a generous piece of dried-apple pie. He was in the habit of thinking aloud as he pondered his cases. This had been his practice for many years—the long, lean years of solitude during which he had subsisted primarily on cold beans on toast, until Mrs. Mack had appeared and taken him in hand. He had not seen fit to change his habits after her arrival, and indeed he had found her to be quite a shrewd judge of character.

She had listened with gratifying interest to the sorry tale of Jack Brody's arrest.

"Where is the child?" she demanded in a tone so fierce it startled a crow sitting on a branch of the wild plum tree outside the open window. The bird answered with an indignant squawk. "Who's looking after the girl?"

The judge swallowed his bite of pie. "Sheriff Morgan left her in the care of the Smirch couple," he replied. "Wasn't much else he could do, under the circumstances."

"Poppycock! I've never heard of anything so ridiculous in all my considerable years! Leaving the poor mite in the care of the very folks who've accused her father. It's preposterous."

Judge Callahan frowned. He couldn't say he disagreed. There was something about the whole business that left him with a deep uneasiness in the pit of his stomach—a pit that was rapidly being filled with Mrs. Mack's fine pie.

"By jingo, I can't seem to make out what all you've flavored it with this time, ma'am. Brown sugar . . . a wee bit of molasses, if I'm not mistaken . . . and nutmeg, that's indisputable. But there's something else, am I right? You can't have gotten your hands on any cinnamon, can you?"

The housekeeper snorted, her eyes—half-moons seamed with wrinkles—crinkling with mirth. Ah, she did love to stump him with her cookery secrets, reflected the judge.

"You needn't waste your wits trying to guess," she replied in her usual tart, high tone. "I reckon you'll need every one of them to put two and two together and come up with four."

Judge Callahan's eyebrows rose. "It's like that, is it?"

he retorted. "Do you mean to tell me you've got it all figured out? You know the truth of the case?"

"It was as plain as pie to me the moment I heard," said the housekeeper archly, her arms crossed over her plump midsection.

"The moment you heard!" the judge sputtered. "Well, let's have it, then. Is Brody guilty or not?"

But Mrs. Mack was sniffing her offended sniff again and refused to enlighten him.

"Far be it from *me*," she humphed, "to interfere with matters of the *law*. Me being just a humble cook and all."

She collected his empty plate and fork and headed for the kitchen, muttering under her breath. *Confounded female,* thought the judge. *Touchier than a porcupine with poison ivy.*

Her shrill voice rang out from the kitchen above the clatter of dishes, eliciting another startled squawk from the eavesdropping crow. "As if any fool couldn't see the man is innocent as a May morn!"

"Ah," replied Judge Callahan, "but I'm not any fool." His housekeeper's opinion, no matter how emphatically stated, was not something to base a verdict on. No, this case wanted facts, and answers. If Jack Brody hadn't stolen those goods, then who in tarnation had?

CHAPTER FOUR
No More Spiders in Our Stew

"YOUR PA'S GONNA HANG," SAID WINTHROP SMIRCH. He was a round-cheeked, lanky-haired boy, with two missing teeth and extremely dirty toenails. He was supposed to be gathering buffalo chips for his mother, but instead he and Charlie were pestering Louisa as she gathered the morning's eggs. It was her third day with the Smirches, and each one of them had felt like a month of Sundays. "My ma says so. She says he's a dirty robber and he deserves what he's got comin'."

Louisa's blood was boiling, but she tried to speak calmly. Pa wouldn't like her cussing out a little boy, which was what she felt like doing.

"Your ma is mistaken," she said in what she hoped

was a dignified tone. "There's been a terrible mistake, but my pa'll get it sorted out. The sheriff is probably investigating the matter right this minute."

"Naw," said Winthrop. "He's gonna hang, soon as they round up a jury."

"What do you mean, 'hang'?" asked Charlie, the four-year-old. He groped in his britches pocket and pulled out a stone, cradling it in both hands like it was a precious jewel.

It was just an ordinary creek stone—round and smooth, a creamy pale gray, almost white. Charlie was exceedingly attached to it. Last night he had fallen asleep with it clutched in his grubby fist. It was lost somewhere in the bed by sunup, and Charlie began the day with a frantic, squalling outcry over his missing stone. During the course of a single morning, Louisa had seen that stone dropped into the butter churn, flung into the fire, tucked into a hen's nest "for safe-keeping," kicked into the straw and muck of the barn floor, and poked into Charlie's ear. It had occurred to Louisa that if Mrs. Smirch could just free them all of the burden of keeping up with that stone, she might not be such a crosspatch. A few more days in its company, and Louisa feared the sourness might settle into her own soul as well.

Of course, putting up with Winthrop wasn't helping matters.

"Hangin's what they do to robbers," he explained to Charlie. "They put a rope around your neck and drop you, and then you're dead. They're gonna hang Louisa's pa, and I'm gonna go watch."

"Winthrop Smirch!" cried an outraged voice. "You take that back!"

Jessamine came flying out of the house, her straggly braids flapping behind her. She rushed up to Winthrop and stood quivering before him, her brown eyes dark with fury.

"You take it back," she repeated. "That's a mean, hateful thing to say, and I won't stand for it."

Winthrop scowled up at her, his pale eyes wide. He reminded Louisa of his pa, with that half-sullen, half-trapped expression. Mr. Smirch had looked just the same way when he and the sheriff rode into the barnyard to arrest Pa.

"Ma said so," Winthrop said uncertainly. "I'm a-tellin' her you hollered at me."

"You go right ahead," said Jessamine, putting her bony hands on her hips. "I don't care what you tell her, so long as you don't say awful things to Louisa. She's our *guest*, you know," she added witheringly, but her scorn seemed lost on Winthrop.

"She ain't no guest," he retorted. "She's a bother, I heard Ma say so."

Louisa spun on her heel and stalked away from the little boy. He was just repeating what his mother had said, anyhow. *Might as well be mad at a calf for mooing,* that's what Pa would say.

Jessamine hurried after her.

"Don't you mind him," she said earnestly, trotting up beside Louisa. "Or Aunt Mattie, neither. She's an old crosspatch, that's all. My ma never liked her, only she was too polite to say so. Seeing as how she was married to Pa's brother and all."

"Did you know her before your parents . . . before you came to live here?" Louisa asked. She was still walking fast, not going anywhere in particular, just wanting to get far away from the Smirch house. Mrs. Smirch would probably tear into her for wandering off, but Louisa didn't care. She had worked her tail off all day, trying to show Mrs. Smirch she was a decent person and a good housekeeper. Why, she'd been keeping house for her pa since she was knee-high to a grasshopper. Her own ma had died when she was barely old enough to remember.

Tell you one thing, Louisa thought, *I keep my floor a sight cleaner than Mrs. Smirch does. Fresher straw ticks, too.* Her skin still felt prickly all over from trying to sleep on that threadbare slab of sacking with bits of straw poking through every which way.

"I never saw her till I come here," said Jessamine. "But my ma was at their wedding. That was back east in Illinois, before Uncle Malcolm took a notion to homestead out here. My ma said Aunt Matilda ain't never had a kind word for nobody in her life. Said if the angel Gabriel flew into her kitchen, Aunt Mattie'd complain that his halo was shining too bright and hurting her eyes."

Louisa chuckled. She wouldn't have thought anyone could make her laugh while her pa was in jail, but Jessamine had a way of saying the sort of things that Louisa herself would have been embarrassed to be caught *thinking*.

"Your ma sounds nice," she said.

Jessamine's eyes grew sorrowful. "She was, she was awful nice. My pa too, and Johnny—"

Her words choked off. Louisa felt stupid. Why'd she go and remind a little orphan girl of her ma? *I ought to know better,* she thought.

But Jessamine was already sparkling again, tugging at Louisa's hand.

"Come on, we're nearly there!" she urged.

"Nearly where?" asked Louisa.

"At the hazel grove! I want to show you that hole. I hope we see him."

This again. Louisa suppressed a smile. Jessamine sure had a lively imagination.

The hazel grove was hardly big enough to deserve its name: just seven or eight hazelnut bushes in a little hollow near the creek, ringed by sturdy, wide-branching cottonwoods—the biggest cottonwoods in the county, Pa said. The grove, which belonged to Mr. Smirch, was something of a local wonder. Every year it produced sweet, delicious hazelnuts in such abundance that Pa said it was near miraculous, considering hazel bushes didn't usually grow in this part of the world.

We had 'em all over County Cork, back in Ireland, where your ma and I grew up, Pa had told Louisa. *Our mothers used to send us out to fill our pails. Your ma had the knack o' shakin' a bush just right so the ripe nuts would clatter to the ground but the green ones would hold tight.*

Mr. Smirch had always traded sacks of hazelnuts for some of Pa's turnips and potatoes. Except for the lush grove, the Smirch land was poor; Mr. Smirch's wheat was scant and his potatoes shriveled. Potatoes were a lot more filling than hazelnuts in a long, hungry winter.

"Here it is," said Jessamine, squatting beside a large

gray rock between two of the hazel bushes. "See the hole there?"

Louisa nodded. It was a good-size hole, all right, big enough for a fox or maybe a badger. She guessed that's what Jessamine had seen, a big old badger with his white chin fur looking like whiskers and his hunched shape like a bag thrown over a shoulder. Though what on earth Jessamine had mistaken for the pointy hat, Louisa couldn't fathom. That part must have been what Pa would call an "embellishment." Pa was mighty fond of a good tale. He'd like Jessamine, if he ever got out of jail.

When he gets out, Louisa corrected herself sternly. Pa'd soon set things straight, if the sheriff stood still long enough to listen to him. Though it did look bad, Louisa had to admit—Mr. Smirch finding his hatchet and all those other things stashed in the old dugout. No one had set foot in that dugout in years, to the best of Pa's knowledge.

If Mr. Smirch hadn't brought the boys with him when he came to borrow Pa's hatchet because he'd misplaced his own, nobody would have had any idea the old deserted dugout was filled with *things*. Winthrop and Charlie had run up the path to play while Pa and Mr. Smirch chatted. The dugout was built into the side of a hill near the creek, looking out over the expanse of Pa's land. Its door was half-hidden by morning glories and tall grass; Louisa hardly ever noticed it at all. They had moved out of the small earthen shelter into their frame house when Louisa was little; she could barely remember living there at all.

Nosy Winthrop had found his way into the dugout and come back to the barnyard jabbering that someone lived there and they had a china doll just like his ma's.

"What's that?" Pa had asked, puzzled. "Ain't no one been in that old place since my wife died. She used to use it for storin' potatoes, but the critters kept gettin' in."

Curious, Pa, Mr. Smirch, and Louisa had walked up the hill to see what Winthrop was going on about. Louisa would never forget the look on Mr. Smirch's face when he saw all the things laid out in that small, dim room.

"That there's my hatchet," he'd said in a low, grim voice. "And that's my clock, and—I'll be durned if that ain't my pocketwatch. It's been missin' for months!" He turned toward Pa, his face suffused with a terrible red anger. "What in thunder are you playin' at, Brody?"

Pa had looked utterly bewildered. "I'm as flummoxed as you are, Malcolm. I had no idea all this was here. I can't imagine who—" He'd turned toward Louisa then in sudden alarm. "Louisa? You know anything about this? Tell the truth now, darlin'."

"That there's my hatchet," he'd said in a low, grim voice. "And that's my clock, and—I'll be durned if that ain't my pocketwatch. It's been missin' for months!"

"No, Pa!" Louisa had cried. "I haven't been in here since I was Winthrop's age, honest!"

Pa studied her face for a long moment, then nodded.

"I don't know what to tell you, Malcolm," he'd said, his voice calm again. "It wasn't me, and it wasn't my daughter, and I'm as confounded as you are to see all these things on my property. There's somethin' mighty strange goin' on here, that's certain."

"What's *strange*," said Mr. Smirch, his voice as cold as a January pond, "is findin' out that a man you thought was honest and a friend is a liar and a thief."

He'd stomped off then, half dragging Charlie and Winthrop by the hands. Pa called after him, but Mr. Smirch never once looked back. That had been Monday. On Wednesday, he'd shown up with the sheriff.

Now it was Friday, and Louisa ought to be home doing her Friday housecleaning. Instead, here she was with Jessamine, staring at a badger hole.

"I wonder," Jessamine was saying. "I wonder if we could fit inside. See how it looks like it opens up bigger once you get past the rock? I'm of half a mind to—"

"Jessamine!" cried Louisa in alarm. "You can't go crawling into holes like that! A badger could tear up a little thing like you."

"But there ain't no badger," insisted Jessamine. "Else

the little old thing in the hat wouldn't go in there."

Louisa sighed in exasperation. "Well, then listen. You crawl in that hole, you're going to muddy up your dress something awful. And then your aunt Matilda will have your hide."

Jessamine's mouth twisted to one side. "Yeah," she said reluctantly. "I s'pose that's true."

"Tell you what. Why don't we sit here in the shade awhile and watch for him? Maybe if we're quiet enough, he won't notice us. Like gopher-hunting."

Jessamine nodded. She pressed her lips tightly together as if she were afraid words would leap out against her will. She pointed to the foot of one of the trees, where there was a shady dimple in the ground. The girls settled themselves on the sparse grass beneath the tree, Jessamine never taking her eyes off the badger's hole.

After a while Louisa guessed the silence was too much for the little girl. "What really happened, Louisa?" Jessamine whispered. "If you don't mind my asking. I'm sure your pa's innocent if you say he is, 'cause you wouldn't be so nice if your pa was a thief. But someone had to put all that stuff in your old dugout, right? Aunt Matilda says it was full to the rafters with stolen goods."

"There aren't any rafters in a dugout," Louisa said, but her sharpness was for Mrs. Smirch, not for Jessamine. "I don't reckon I know how those things got there. Nor my pa, neither. We haven't used that dugout since I was littler than Winthrop. My pa built the cabin when I was four years old. We were only in the dugout till he saved up enough for lumber for a frame house."

She remembered, faintly, how excited Ma had been when they moved into the frame house. *No more spiders in our stew, Louisa,* she had said, whirling around in the wide new room. Pa hadn't gotten the roof on yet, and Ma said she almost wished it could stay like that. *The sky for our roof, there's nothing grander than that,* she'd declared, and Pa had laughed and spun her around the open room in a waltz. That was one of the last clear memories Louisa had of her ma. It was a good one. Her skirts billowing out like sheets on a line, her hair tumbling out of its coils, her laughing eyes looking into Pa's.

Louisa never felt sad, thinking of her ma. She'd been so little when ma took sick. But now there was a little gnawing thing inside her wondering if she was going to lose Pa, too, and have nothing left of him but memories.

"It's a mystery," said Jessamine softly, her eyes on the hole again. "Maybe there's a gang of outlaws hiding out somewhere and that's where they were stashing their loot." She snorted. "Or maybe Aunt Mattie did it herself. Maybe she was aiming to go and set up house-keeping there all by herself. She's always saying how one day she's just going to up and leave the pack of us ungrateful wretches, and then we'll see how we like it." She giggled. "I think I'd like it pretty well."

Chapter Five
Evangeline

No creature—either with a hat or without one—ever did make an appearance in the hazel grove, and finally the girls had to head back to the house. They knew Mrs. Smirch would be madder than a wet hen, and she was.

"I knew *you* was likely to be a shirker," she said to Louisa, waggling her ladle at Louisa, "but Jessamine Henry, you ought to know better! What would your poor ma say if she knew you'd taken to runnin' off in the middle of the afternoon when there's chores to be done?"

Jessamine's mouth opened and closed right back again. Louisa knew exactly how she felt. There were so many things you wanted to say—or shout—when Mrs.

Smirch lit into you like that, and you couldn't. Because as bad as her tongue-lashings were, they were only the beginning of what Mrs. Smirch could do to make a person's life miserable, and both girls knew it. Louisa reached over and squeezed Jessamine's hand. Whatever happened with Pa, Louisa was only stuck with the Smirches for a short while. Jessamine was there forever. Or until she grew up, at least.

Mrs. Smirch berated the girls for a little while longer, then ordered Jessamine to watch the boys and Louisa to chop some carrots for the stew.

"Mind you don't go pocketin' any of my carrots, now, you hear me?" she added contemptuously. "I reckon I know your thievin' ways."

"I'm not a thief!" Louisa burst out. She couldn't help it. As if she'd go stealing carrots!

"Don't you sass me, girl," snapped Mrs. Smirch. "Apple don't far fall from the tree."

"My pa didn't take your things," Louisa said through gritted teeth.

Mrs. Smirch snorted. "Well, my grandmother's windup clock didn't walk to your pa's dugout all by itself. Nor my husband's hatchet, nor his pocketwatch, nor my china-head doll that I toted in my own lap all the way from Topeka in case the Lord ever sent me a girl-child.

Never thought I'd see my poor doll again." She sniffed as if still mourning the loss of the doll that was now slumping crazily on the mantel, next to the windup clock that didn't seem to have been wound or set since its return. "I'm missin' a whole sack of carded wool, too. Lord knows where your pa stashed *it*."

"Nowhere!" insisted Louisa. "I don't know who took your things, but I assure you it wasn't my pa!"

Mrs. Smirch rolled her eyes. "Oh, you *assure* me, do you? Well, Miss How-de-do-and-la-di-da, ain't no use your puttin' on airs—don't change the fact that your pa's bound for the hot place!"

Tears stung Louisa's eyes, and she quickly turned away. A pile of carrots lay awaiting her on the table next to the big chopping knife. She slammed the knife through a carrot, lopping off the skinny tip. Chopping felt good. She could think of several things she'd like to chop right about now, and carrots were pretty low on the list.

Mrs. Smirch watched her suspiciously a minute and then, apparently satisfied that Louisa wasn't going to come after her with the knife, picked up a basket of mending and went outside to sit in the shade of the north wall, where there was a bit of a breeze. Between the late-summer sun and the hot stove, the house was stifling.

Jessamine was outside trying to keep Charlie from throwing his precious white stone at the chickens. Now and then Louisa could see glimpses of them through the open door. The little girl looked worn out, her braids slapping her back as she ran after the boys. Louisa had a sudden urge to fix those straggly braids, comb the hair smooth and plait them neatly, like Jessamine's ma probably used to do, like Louisa's own ma had done for her when she was little.

Mrs. Smirch's ugly words were still stinging in Louisa's head. She hadn't been putting on airs. Pa liked her to speak properly. He said her ma always sounded like someone out of a book, and he meant that as a compliment. Pa wasn't a learned man himself, but he had great respect for book-learning. He owned two books, a Bible and a volume of poems by Mr. Henry Wadsworth Longfellow, and whenever he had a spare minute he read one of those books. He always read out loud so Louisa wouldn't be left out. He liked some passages so well, she knew them by heart. His favorite lines were the ones about the simple farmers whose "dwellings were open as day and the hearts of the owners"—

There the richest was poor, and the poorest lived in abundance.

She thought of that book sitting on the little round table beside Pa's chair, in their own simple dwelling, which really did seem as open as day, as open as Pa's big heart, especially compared to the shut-tight heart of Mrs. Smirch. Louisa was overcome with a fierce longing to go home. Mr. Smirch hadn't given her much time to pack. He'd told her gruffly to fetch what clothes she needed, and she'd been so shocked by Pa's arrest that she hadn't thought to take anything more than that. She ought to have brought Pa's book, at least, and her picture of Ma and Pa on their wedding day, Pa all stiff and starched in his new suit, and Ma with her hair swept high and held in place by a tortoiseshell comb, the only fancy thing she'd ever owned. Pa had given that comb to Louisa on her twelfth birthday. He said she had hair just like her mother's. The comb was tucked safely into a little wooden box on Louisa's dresser at home, waiting for her to be grown-up enough to put up her hair.

Home. Louisa yearned to be back home, with Pa and their books and things, and their cow, Evangeline, who was named after one of Mr. Longfellow's poems.

Evangeline! Louisa's breath caught in her throat at the sudden, terrible thought. *The livestock! They'll die with no one to look after them. Evangeline will have the milk sickness if I don't go milk her. And the chickens—*

The knife fell out of Louisa's hand as she realized she hadn't even put the chickens in their coop before she left. Foxes and owls had likely gotten them all the very first night.

Without thinking about what she was doing, still clutching half a carrot in one hand, she sprinted out of the house and cut across the Smirches' pasture, headed for home. Mrs. Smirch, patching Winthrop's breeches in her shady spot on the far side of the house, didn't see her go.

CHAPTER SIX
What in Tarnation?

HOME WAS TWO MILES AWAY. LOUISA FOLLOWED
Spitwhistle Creek upstream, skirting the stands of wind-
twisted cottonwood that fringed the bank. Her feet
pounded on the buffalo grass, echoing her heart. She
shoved all thoughts of the Smirches to the back of her
mind. Surely they'd understand she couldn't let her pa's
stock die. Anybody'd have to understand that.

After a long time the creek swung east in a curve
she recognized. Home was just over the next rise. A
rough-legged hawk was wheeling in the sky right over
where she figured the chickenyard would be, and her
heart lurched. Would there be any hens left alive? Must
be at least one, she guessed, or that hawk wouldn't bother.

She cut through Pa's cornfield, the silken tassels whispering all around her. Pa'd been out harvesting that corn when the sheriff came. It needed to be gotten into the barn before the critters got it, or there'd be some hungry bellies on the place that winter. Pa just had to get home soon, he had to.

On the other side of the field she jumped the little crawfish brook that cut across Pa's land to Spitwhistle Creek, and she hurried to the barn. She listened for Evangeline's mooing, but the place was eerily quiet.

I'm too late, she thought miserably. Suddenly she wasn't hurrying at all. Slowly she walked the last few steps. Now she could hear something, a terrible sound, a sound of faint, pitiful sighs, over and over. The last dying breaths of a poor neglected cow, it must be, and suddenly Louisa could not move. She was terrified to round the corner and look inside the barn.

What she saw, when she did look, made her scream and jump backward.

"What in tarnation?" yelled Mr. Smirch, starting to his feet and knocking over a pail of milk. Evangeline turned a languid eye toward him, unconcerned by the commotion.

"What are you doin' here, girl?" bellowed the big farmer.

Louisa gaped at him, dumbfounded. "I . . . I got to worrying about the livestock," she faltered. "I thought they'd starve. I didn't know you were looking after them."

Mr. Smirch blinked. Louisa thought he looked almost embarrassed.

"'Course I wasn't goin' to let them starve," he muttered. "What kind of fool do you take me for?"

"I didn't know," said Louisa again.

Mr. Smirch looked away, frowning. He set the milk pail upright and stood there staring at the white liquid turning dark in the dirt.

"I ain't done the hens yet," he said at last. "Why don't you go hunt the eggs, long as you're here. Then you better scoot back to my place. I don't reckon you asked leave of my missus before you lit out." He cocked her a sidelong glance. Louisa shook her head, blushing.

"Yes, sir," she said meekly, turning toward the hen-house. Then she thought of something and turned back. "Mr. Smirch, sir? Would it be all right if I went in the house for a minute? I—" She groped for an excuse. "I'd like to get my sourdough starter and bring it back to your place. I need to add to it now and then or it'll peter out." She saw his lips press together again and added hastily, "Anyway, I need a basket for the eggs."

"Fine," he growled. "You just be quick, hear?"

"Yes, sir."

The house was stuffy inside from having been shut up all day. She pushed through a wall of heat into the big silent space that was sitting room, kitchen, and Pa's bedroom all in one. Everything seemed strange, not quite the way she remembered it, as if she'd been gone a lot longer than just a few days. But nothing had changed, of course. This was home. Here Ma and Pa had whirled in their sky-ceilinged ballroom. Here was where Pa's smoky voice recited poetry of an evening. He had loved the cadences of Mr. Longfellow's verses, and the pictures they painted.

> *This is the forest primeval. The murmuring*
> *pines and the hemlocks,*
> *Bearded with moss, and in garments green,*
> *indistinct in the twilight,*
> *Stand like Druids of eld, with voices sad*
> *and prophetic,*
> *Stand like harpers hoar, with beards that*
> *rest on their bosoms.*

"Ain't no one ever wrote quite like him," Pa would say. "He tells grand stories, like that old Greek fellow,

Homer—but he tells 'em in words that trip off the tongue like a good Irish lay. I reckon it's because he's American, like we are, Louisa. All these people from different parts o' the world comin' together here to make a new life, mixin' up their food and songs and ways o' doing things. Ah, 'tis a fine land you've been born to, Louisa Brody. Full o' possibility."

Oh, Pa. Louisa shook herself back to the present and fetched a large basket from the lean-to. She tucked Pa's Longfellow book in the bottom, and the wedding picture, and the jar of sourdough starter wrapped in a rag. Then she went to her little bedroom at the south end of the house. Pa had built it with windows on two walls so she could see the sun come up in the morning and watch it sink into the prairie at night, burning the wide sky all golden and pink. She'd shoved most of her clothes into a poke when Mr. Smirch told her she had to go to his place, so there wasn't much left in the room besides the bed and the dresser. She saw her knitting needles poking out of the rolled-up end of a sock she was making for Pa and decided to stuff that in the basket as well, along with a ball of red wool for the second sock.

Then she moved to the dresser. Atop it sat the little polished wooden box that held her mother's tortoiseshell comb. She wanted it with her now, in case . . . she didn't want to think of what kind of "in case" there might be. *I just ought to have it with me, that's all,* she thought. She lifted the cover off the wooden box.

The comb wasn't there.

CHAPTER SEVEN

The Seven-Day Clock

MRS. SMIRCH STARTED RAILING AT LOUISA BEFORE she even got through the cabin door with her basket of eggs and treasures, but Louisa was too numb inside to take in much of what she was saying. All she could think of was her ma's missing comb. It was the only thing she had that belonged to her mother, and that ache, sitting on top of the fear for Pa that had churned in her stomach since he was taken away, made her feel like she was going to be sick. Which would only give Mrs. Smirch something else to fuss at her about, she supposed.

Not until that night, when she lay itching and fidgeting in bed alongside the other children, did she have a minute's peace to think things over. Someone had to have taken that comb; someone must have gone into her house after she left and stolen it, just like someone had robbed the Smirches.

"Louisa," whispered Jessamine in the darkness. "Don't let Aunt Mattie get under your skin. She just ain't happy 'less she's got something to fuss about."

"It isn't that," Louisa murmured, and she told Jessamine about the comb.

Jessamine gasped and would have sat bolt upright if Louisa hadn't shoved her back against the straw tick.

"But don't you see?" Jessamine whispered. "That's proof your pa didn't do it, just like you said! There's got to be a real robber around, and soon as your house was empty, he went in and helped himself. Was anything else missing?"

"I don't think so," said Louisa. But she knew she hadn't looked too closely the short while she was in the house. She closed her eyes and pictured home, tried to recall if there'd been anything missing. She remembered how it had felt strange, as if she'd been gone a lot longer than just a few nights. But there hadn't been anything different, had there? Pa's books on the table, the wedding picture on the shelf, her sewing basket in the corner. The room all hushed and lonely, like it missed her and Pa.

"Wait a minute," she said suddenly, forgetting to

keep her voice low. Jessamine shushed her and Winthrop muttered in his sleep, rolling over, scissoring his legs. Louisa waited for him to settle and then whispered, "Our clock was gone. I didn't hear it ticking."

"Sure it hadn't just run down?" asked Jessamine, but even in a whisper her voice had a trembly excitement. Louisa knew they were thinking the same thing. The Smirches' clock had been stolen too, and Mr. Smirch's pocketwatch. Could it be this thief, whoever he was, had a hankering for timepieces?

"It couldn't have run down," she said. "It's a seven-day clock. I wind it on Sundays. Today's only Friday."

"You girls cut out that yammerin' afore you wake my boys!" screeched Mrs. Smirch from the other room, rapping on the wall with what could only be that infernal ladle. Jessamine clapped a hand over her mouth to stifle a giggle, and even with the worry over her pa and the comb and everything, Louisa had to grin too. Mrs. Smirch was louder than a rooster at sunup—a rooster at sunup having his tail feathers pulled out.

CHAPTER EIGHT

The Badger Hole

FOR THE NEXT FEW DAYS, MRS. SMIRCH KEPT SUCH a sharp eye on Louisa that she could hardly get away to use the privy, much less slip home to see if anything else was missing. She had tried to tell Mr. Smirch (because for all he was so gruff and taciturn, he was at least nice enough to hike the two miles each way to milk Evangeline and feed the hens every day, and in the middle of his wheat harvest, too), but he brushed off her suggestions.

"Ain't no thief skulkin' around your Pa's place," he said. "If'n there was, he'd-a helped himself to the milk cow first, not go foolin' with combs and whatnot." He was striding away from her before he even finished the sentence. "That there's a mighty fine cow," she heard him mutter as he disappeared into the barn.

Bet that's the only reason you're looking after her, thought Louisa darkly. *You figure you can just keep her after they hang—* She couldn't finish the thought. *Oh, Pa.*

Finally there came an afternoon when Mrs. Smirch had either decided Louisa was cowed enough not to run off, or she was just so tired of Winthrop and Charlie's squabbling that she didn't care.

"You girls take them boys outside for a while," she ordered. "Take a bucket with you. Might as well go see if any nuts have dropped in the grove."

Jessamine shot Louisa an excited glance. Louisa knew she was still hankering after another glimpse of her hat-wearing badger.

Mrs. Smirch was eyeing the girls suspiciously. "None of your tricks, now," she said to Louisa. "Don't you even think of draggin' my young'uns all the way to your place, and you best not leave 'em neither. Any harm comes to them boys, I'll have your hide."

"Yes, ma'am," said Louisa meekly. *As if I'd ever dream of letting those little terrors loose in my house.* There wasn't anything safe from being pawed and prodded if Winthrop and Charlie were around. At least, if they weren't busy fighting with each other. Winthrop was a teaser, and

Charlie a biter. And when he wasn't biting, Charlie was crying. But that, Louisa reflected, may have been because Winthrop was either pinching him, pelting him with pebbles, or sitting on him—sometimes all three at once.

But today the boys seemed glad to be out in the wind, running barefoot across the prairie, war-whooping and jumping over prairie-dog holes. They raced toward the hazel grove and the girls hurried behind, hard-pressed to keep up.

"Ain't no chance we'll see him today," said Jessamine, her mouth twisting in disappointment. "Them boys'll scare off every living creature 'tween here and Fletcher."

Louisa smiled at her in sympathy. She knew Jessamine's heart was set on proving she really had seen what she said she'd seen. Louisa knew how it felt to be dead sure of something, sure right down to your bones, and have folks scoff at you for it.

"Maybe it'll be curious and come see what all the ruckus is," she said soothingly. Jessamine's eyes went all twinkly again. Seemed like the least little kind word made her blossom like a prairie rose after a good rain.

Winthrop and Charlie thundered into the hazel grove, crushing a good many nuts under their heels as they ran. Louisa didn't know how they could stand it. Her feet were pretty tough from going barefoot all summer, but prairie grass was one thing, and hazel shells quite another. She scooped up a couple of cracked hulls and picked out the tasty nutmeat inside.

"If these were walnuts," she mused, "we could make ink out of the shells. My pa told me how to do it. I don't think it works with hazelnut shells, though."

"Can you write?" asked Jessamine. "I was learning how, before I came here. I can read pretty well. But Aunt Mattie says schooling is a waste of time for orphan girls."

"Oh, that's just silly," said Louisa. "Everybody needs to know how to write a letter, don't they? My pa says reading and writing are as important as knowing how to cook, sew, shoe a horse, and plow a furrow."

The eager light was shining in Jessamine's eyes again. "Oh, Louisa! Supposing you was to teach me to write! Would you? We could make some ink somehow, couldn't we?"

Louisa nodded. "I suppose so. But what would we write on? I've got paper at home, but . . ." There was no point in her trying to slip away home again. Mrs. Smirch wasn't ever going to let her out alone.

"What about those flat stones by the creek?" Jessamine asked. "You know, over yonder past the Hole." She spoke the word almost reverently, pointing. "Where *he* lives." Then she jumped to her feet, shrieking.

"Charlie, you get out of there! Winthrop, pull him out!"

She pelted toward the badger's hole, Louisa close on her heels. Charlie was on his hands and knees crawling into the hole, just his dirty feet sticking out. Winthrop was urging him on.

"Go on, I'm a-comin' right behind you. Don't be afraid, you gutless—"

"Winthrop!" Louisa's voice was stern. "Don't you encourage him! Grab his ankles before he gets any farther!"

"Naw, I wanna see where it goes," said Winthrop, giving Charlie's bottom a shove. A muffled yelp came from inside the hole. "Might be a cave under there with gold and jewels and stuff."

"Ain't no gold mine!" scoffed Jessamine. "It's the entrance to a home. Someone *lives* there!"

"Maybe a badger," interjected Louisa, shooting Jessamine a warning glance. The last thing they needed was for Winthrop to think some strange little bearded man lived at the end of that tunnel. He'd never rest until he got in there to see for himself. She pushed Winthrop aside and grabbed hold of Charlie's feet.

"I'm tellin'!" Winthrop howled, and Charlie let loose with an outraged howl of his own as Louisa yanked him backward.

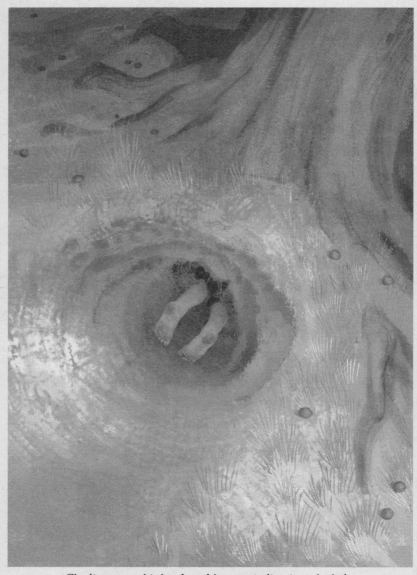

Charlie was on his hands and knees crawling into the hole,
just his dirty feet sticking out.

She pulled so hard that she tumbled backward herself, landing painfully on a tree root. Charlie fell half on top of her, his face smacking against the ground. Winthrop laughed and jeered. Jessamine knelt to help little Charlie to his feet. He was wailing loud enough to curdle milk.

"Hush, honey," Louisa said, feigning more affection that she felt at the moment. "Are you hurt?"

"I think he's all right," Jessamine called above the blubbering. "Winthrop, you better hush up."

"Ha, look at his face!" guffawed Winthrop. "You look like you done took a bath in dirt, Charlie!"

"My white stone!" Charlie wailed. "I lost my white stone!"

"Oh, Lord," said Jessamine wearily. "Not again."

"I need to get it," Charlie insisted. His face had a stormy, thinking-about-biting look.

Louisa bit her lip, wondering what on earth she was supposed to do. She couldn't let Charlie go back in, that was certain. She'd have to do it herself. Charlie's wails were escalating in volume. If there were some kind of critter inside that hole, Charlie was going to rouse it for sure.

"Hush, Charlie. I'll try. Maybe it didn't go in too far. But you have to be quiet."

Charlie's howls subsided to whimpers. Louisa crouched low in front of the hole, peering at the dark ground inside, hunting against hope for a gleam of not-exactly-white. Right away she knew it was going to be hopeless. She'd never be able to see one little rock in that dark earthen tunnel. Cautiously she put a hand inside and felt around on the smooth, hardpacked dirt. Nothing.

"I'll have to go in a little way," she said. Though she was quailing inside, she eased forward into the tunnel on her hands and knees. It smelled cool and dusty, not rank like she expected an animal burrow to smell. That was some small comfort, at least. Maybe it was abandoned. But no, Jessamine was certain she had seen something go into that hole.

"Didja find it?" demanded Charlie behind her.

"Hush," she hissed. She heard Jessamine warning Winthrop not to even *think* of smacking Louisa in the behind with his stick—which of course meant that Winthrop had been thinking of doing that very thing. Louisa was grateful to Jessamine for sparing her the wallop. She crept forward a tiny bit more, groping, groping . . . and then she froze, her heart turning to lead inside her.

She was staring right into a pair of eyes. Little round eyes, shining in the darkness, looking right back at her. What kind of creature they belonged to, she couldn't tell.

But one thing was certain: they were not the eyes of a badger.

She was staring right into a pair of eyes. Little round eyes,
shining in the darkness, looking right back at her.

CHAPTER NINE
The White Stone

LOUISA DIDN'T DARE MOVE. PA SAID A WILD CRITTER would lunge at you if you made any quick motions. *Slow and easy—that's the way to back out of a tight spot.* Louisa was afraid to move at all. The voices of the children behind her seemed suddenly very far away. Her body was blocking the daylight, and in the dark tunnel she couldn't make out more than a shadowy shape around those curious, staring eyes.

She could hear it breathing. Whatever it was—a fox? A bobcat? No, cats didn't live in underground dens—whatever it was, it had a funny, faint whistle in its breath. Not a snuffle or a growl, but a gentle fluty sound a little like Charlie's snoring. And those eyes. They had expression; the gaze was intelligent and scrutinizing, almost—Louisa felt silly thinking it—stern. Now what kind of critter, she wondered, looked at you *sternly* when you poked your head into its den?

Her eyes were adjusting to the gloom, and she began to make out the shape of the critter's body. The tunnel was wider than she would have guessed, much bigger than a fox would need. A squat, rounded shape filled the space, a compact bulk that did not seem fuzzy or furry at the edges the way it should. And above the eyes . . . *But that can't be,* Louisa thought, wishing desperately she had a light.

If she didn't know better, she could swear the critter's shape tapered to a tall point above its eyes.

"Louisa!" wailed Charlie behind her. He was smacking her on the back, and it hurt. "You find it yet?"

Louisa held her breath, terrified the critter would pounce. But it held its ground, simply staring. Ever so slowly she edged herself backward. Somehow she had to get out of that tunnel without provoking an attack. Her neck and shoulders ached, and the hard ground was hurting her knees. She scooched another inch backward.

Then she gasped and froze again. The critter had moved. It had taken a step toward her, she was sure of it. Her backward creeping had shifted her just enough to let in a smidgen of daylight, and she could see that the critter was reaching out toward her with its paw—no, not a paw: it was hairless and pale. She shuddered, fearing her heart would burst. Behind her Jessamine was calling out her name, and the boys were clamoring. The thing that wasn't a paw extended toward her, opening flat.

It was a hand.

And upon its palm lay Charlie's white stone.

CHAPTER TEN
A Critter with Hands

PA'S ADVICE UTTERLY FORGOTTEN, LOUISA SCRAMBLED backward out of the hole. Her breath came in ragged, panicky gasps. She felt dizzy. She collided with someone behind her—Charlie, from the sound of the wails—and before she had a chance to untangle herself, something came sailing out of the tunnel, landing with a soft plunk in the dirt between her hands.

Charlie's stone.

That critter had tossed Charlie's stone to her, as if it had known exactly what she was looking for.

A critter with hands like a human being. And—she could no longer deny what she'd seen with her own eyes—a pointed hat.

"My white stone!" Charlie crowed, diving for the precious rock. Louisa started to her feet, never taking her eyes off the tunnel's entrance.

"Louisa, what is it?" cried Jessamine. "You look like you done seen a ghost."

"Not a ghost," murmured Louisa, and slowly she turned to look at the other girl. "I saw something," she whispered so Winthrop wouldn't hear, "but *it wasn't a ghost.*"

Jessamine stared at her uncomprehendingly for a moment, then gasped, her mouth falling open.

"You mean—"

"Yes," said Louisa, looking back at the hole. There was no sign of the . . . the whatever-it-was.

Before Louisa could stop her, Jessamine had dropped to her knees before the tunnel's entrance.

"No!" Louisa cried, and Winthrop crowded close.

"Whatcha lookin' for?" he demanded. "You see somethin' in there, Louisa?"

"I found Charlie's stone," Louisa said hastily, avoiding the question. "Here, Charlie. Now come on, Jessamine, we'd better get back."

She was afraid Jessamine would put up a fuss, but the younger girl rose to her feet, nodding.

"Yes, let's get on back," she said. Her eyes were very bright.

Clutching his stone, Charlie broke into a run, threading his way back through the trees. Winthrop raced behind him, waving his stick. Louisa lingered for one last cautious glance at the hole. There was nothing to be seen.

But Jessamine clutched her hand.

"I saw him," she whispered. "The one I told you about. And, Louisa—" She looked up at the older girl, her eyes wide with awe. "He put a finger to his lips, like he was saying to shush. He didn't want me to let the boys know he was there."

Watching Winthrop chase Charlie with his stick swishing through the air dangerously close to the smaller boy's head, Louisa didn't blame the little man one bit.

If he *was* a man. What kind of person lived in a hole under the ground? He was too small to be human— smaller even than a human child. He couldn't have been more than a foot high. But what else could he be? Animals didn't wear clothes and hats, and have beards, and have hands with fingers and everything. An animal wouldn't know how to say *shhh* by putting a finger to its lips.

Of all the strange things that had happened to

Louisa in the past few days, this was by far the strangest.

The children were halfway home when Jessamine stopped short, clapping a hand to her head.

"The hazelnuts!" she cried in dismay.

Louisa groaned. In all the excitement, she had clean forgotten about collecting nuts for Mrs. Smirch.

"We left the basket in the grove," Jessamine added.

Charlie's short legs had grown tired by this time, and he was dragging along, holding Jessamine's hand. Even Winthrop looked hot and weary; the sun was high overhead now, and the pleasant morning cool had given way to a shimmering August heat.

"You'd better take the boys on home," said Louisa. "I'll go back for the nuts."

Jessamine looked as though she wanted to protest— Louisa knew she was hoping for another glimpse of the strange little man—but Charlie was pulling on Jessamine's hand, whining.

"C'mon, Jessie, let's go!" he urged. "I want my dinner."

Jessamine sighed and nodded. "All right. But, Louisa . . ." She dropped her voice, giving Louisa's arm a last squeeze. "Be sure to tell me if anything happens."

"I will," Louisa promised. "But I'm just going to fill up the nut pail and come straight back. I don't want your aunt Mattie thinking I went home again."

Jessamine let Charlie tug her over the grass toward his home. Winthrop trudged behind them. Louisa watched them for a moment, then turned and hurried back to the hazel grove. She knew Jessamine had hoped for another encounter with the—the *thing*, but Louisa rather hoped he'd disappeared far down his tunnel. Too much had happened; she needed time to sit and think about all this. In all the stories Pa had ever told her, he'd never mentioned a word about little old bearded fellows who lived in burrows under the prairie. Louisa aimed to just fill up that pail with nuts and scoot back to the Smirches quick as fire. As it was, she was going to be late for the midday meal, and Mrs. Smirch would have something else to fuss at her about.

She approached the trees, slowing warily, looking for the little man. There was no sight of him. The grove was deserted. There was the pail, right in the middle, under a tree. She reached for the handle and got another shock.

The pail was full to the brim with hazelnuts.

CHAPTER ELEVEN

How Softly They Gleamed

LATE IN THE EVENING, MRS. SMIRCH SET THE GIRLS to washing dishes while she wrestled the boys to bed in the other room. Louisa had been waiting all day for a chance to tell Jessamine about that pail of nuts.

"How did he know that's what we came for?" Jessamine asked.

"What else would we bring a pail for?" Louisa shrugged. "Or maybe he heard us talking."

"Oh, Louisa!" Jessamine clasped her hands together, water dripping down her sleeves. "He's awfully nice, ain't he! What do you suppose he is?"

"I haven't the faintest idea," said Louisa fervently. She still had that sense of living in a dream. In the past week, hardly one thing had happened that made any sense to her at all.

"You girls ain't done yet?" asked Mrs. Smirch, coming out from the back room. "You need to hurry up and get to bed."

She sank into her chair by the hearth and reached for her mending basket. Mrs. Smirch was a worker; Louisa had to give her that. The girl still wasn't impressed with the state of Mrs. Smirch's floors, but she supposed Winthrop and Charlie had a lot to do with that.

"Oh, me," sighed Mrs. Smirch, threading a needle. "I'm plumb wore out. Malcolm ain't come in from the barn yet? Louisa, what's that book you been hidin'? I found it in a poke under your nightclothes. I hope it ain't more stolen goods from your pa's dugout."

Louisa's mouth fell open in horror. Mrs. Smirch was going through her things! Of all the indignities she'd had to endure since coming here, this was the worst. To be accused of stealing her pa's own book!

"It's my father's," she said, hastily drying her hands on her apron. She needed to see the book, to reassure herself that Mrs. Smirch hadn't harmed it in any way. "Where is it?"

Mrs. Smirch cocked an eyebrow at her. "Mind your

manners, girl," she said mildly. "Ain't no need to take my head off. Can't blame folks for being a mite suspicious after what they found in your pa's old dugout."

"We don't *know* how those things got there—" began Louisa for the dozenth time.

"Save your breath, child," snapped Mrs. Smirch. "I heard it all before. Now, what I was fixin' to say afore you got all hot and bothered on me was that I'm of a mind to have you read me a little of that there book. I don't reckon it'll do any harm to use it, even if it ain't your'n."

Which is how, some minutes later, Louisa found herself reading Longfellow's poems to Mrs. Smirch, Jessamine, and, when he came in from his barn chores, Mr. Smirch. Mrs. Smirch sat in her rocker, sewing, listening with that same twisted smile. Jessamine sat on the hooked rug before the fire, her hands clasped around her knees, eyes shining, drinking in Louisa's words like they were water after a drought. Even Mr. Smirch seemed to be enjoying the reading; he was hunkered on a bench with a knife and a strip of leather, but his hands had fallen idle and he was staring at the fire, nodding now and then at a turn of phrase he liked.

Fair was she to behold, that maiden of
seventeen summers.

Black were her eyes as the berry that grows
on the thorn by the way-side,
Black, yet how softly they gleamed beneath
the brown shade of her tresses!

It was the most pleasant moment Louisa had known since she first set foot in this house, and for just a minute, all the worries and mysteries that had churned incessantly in her mind for a week subsided, and she felt almost peaceful.

And then Mrs. Smirch pounced.

Chapter Twelve
May as Well Get It Over With

ALL LOUISA DID—SUCH A LITTLE THING—WAS RAISE a hand to scratch her head. She didn't even notice she was scratching until she felt Mrs. Smirch's gaze upon her and looked up to find those sharp eyes watching her narrowly, like the woman was a rattler about to strike. Louisa's voice faltered; her hand fell to the book in her lap, just as Mrs. Smirch thrust aside her sewing and sprang up to inspect the girl's head.

Louisa instinctively recoiled, and Mrs. Smirch hissed at her to hold still. She pushed Louisa's head downward and pawed at her hair, shoving aside the long heavy locks on the girl's neck, scrabbling, scrabbling.

"What is it?" Louisa yelped. "A spider?"

"What in tarnation, Matilda?" asked Mr. Smirch.

"What were you scratchin', girl? I saw you scratch," said Mrs. Smirch. "Hold still so I can get a look at your neck."

An awful chill coursed through Louisa's blood. She knew what Mrs. Smirch was looking for.

"I don't have them," she protested, gasping against the pain of her hair being tugged. "Honest, I don't! I've never had them in my life!"

"Then what," said Mrs. Smirch, and her voice was grimmer than Louisa had ever heard it be before, "do you call *this*?"

She jerked Louisa's head back and brandished something before her eyes. Louisa blinked in pain and shame, rearing away from that pinch-fingered hand.

"I don't see anything," she whispered, but she knew, with a sick certainty, that what Mrs. Smirch was waving at her was too tiny to stick out beyond the pinching forefinger and thumb.

"You . . . got . . . lice!" said Mrs. Smirch, and there was a note of triumph in her voice. "I knew it! Bah!" She smushed the insect between her fingers and flicked it into the fire. "Jessamine, get over here and let me have a look at you."

Jessamine's hand went to her head, her eyes wide

and fearful. Louisa's face burned with shame. Mr. Smirch remained silent, just watching, his lips pressed together in the same old way.

"You brung them filthy critters into my house," muttered Mrs. Smirch, picking through Jessamine's hair, "and now my young'uns is like to get 'em too! I knew I'd rue the day I took you in."

"I tell you, I never had them before!" protested Louisa. She never knew what made her lose her temper—was it hearing little Jessamine squeak in pain when Mrs. Smirch pulled her hair? Was it simply one insult too many? The words were pouring out of her mouth before she had any idea of saying them. "Matter of fact, I bet I got them *here*! Sleeping on that itchy old straw tick! Probably has bedbugs, too!"

A terrible silence fell over the room. Mrs. Smirch stood frozen with her hands in Jessamine's hair, staring at Louisa with astonishment and rage in her eyes. Louisa's breath caught in her throat.

"What's that you said?" asked Mrs. Smirch softly, dangerously.

Louisa couldn't answer.

"You want to walk very carefully here, girl. You're here out of charity, and you'd do well to remember it. If I weren't a softhearted woman, I'd have packed you off a week ago, harvest or no harvest. They can send you to the orphanage in Topeka while your father awaits trial, for all I care."

She resumed her hunt through Jessamine's hair.

"Well, I don't see none," she said, "but that don't mean they ain't there. Hair like yours, it's hard to tell."

She turned a contemplative stare toward Louisa.

"Yours'll have to go," she said matter-of-factly.

Louisa blanched. *No, oh no.*

"Her *hair*?" squealed Jessamine. "Oh, Aunt Mattie, you can't!"

"Got no choice," said Mrs. Smirch. "Can't let 'em overrun the house."

"No, please," whispered Louisa, her hand going to her head. There was no way she was going to let Mrs. Smirch cut off her hair, her long brown hair that Pa said looked just like her mother's.

"I'll get one of those special combs—" she pleaded.

"Where you gonna get a fine-tooth comb, child? Have to go to town for that, and if 'tweren't such a hardship to get you to town right now, you'd be there already and your critters wouldn't be none of my never-mind."

She released her grip on Jessamine's tresses and gestured toward the door.

"Come on, then," she said to Louisa. "May as well

get it over with. Have to do it outside, of course. I'll just get my scissors."

"Please," Louisa repeated, but no one answered. Mrs. Smirch was rummaging through her sewing basket. Mr. Smirch slowly folded up his whittling knife and strode out to the barn.

Tears were rolling down Jessamine's face. She looked as stricken as if it were her own hair about to be cut off.

Louisa met her eyes for a long moment, and then suddenly she was out the door, running as hard as she could.

CHAPTER THIRTEEN
A Goose Indeed

SHE KNEW THEY'D LOOK FOR HER IN HER OWN HOUSE.
Already she could hear Mrs. Smirch hollering for her husband. Louisa knew she'd have to find somewhere to hide.

She thought of the dugout, but she was afraid Mr. Smirch would look there when he didn't find her at home. There were other neighbors to the east, but she wasn't sure of the way. There was no road. The thought of wandering uncertainly across the open prairie in the dark made her shudder.

But where was there to go? She couldn't go back.

I'll go to Pa, she thought. *I'll go to town.*

Follow the creek upstream far enough, she knew, and you'd come to a wide shallow river. Head east along its banks, and sooner or later you'd reach the town of Fletcher. Most likely later—it was a good thirteen miles away.

Thirteen miles. Could she do it? Could she walk that far?

Got no choice.

But she certainly couldn't start out now, after dark, not with wolves and coyotes and who knew what else on the hunt. And she'd need food, water, maybe a blanket.

She figured she could get all those things at home tomorrow, if she watched for her chance. Mr. Smirch couldn't spend the whole day looking for her; he had his wheat to think of. She'd slip in and slip out, and then she'd trek to Fletcher. She'd rather stay in jail with Pa than spend one more day under Mrs. Smirch's cold eye.

Besides, it occurred to her that she had information for the sheriff. The thief, whoever he was, was still on the prowl! The sheriff needed to know about her ma's stolen comb and another missing clock. Louisa felt heartened, now that she had a plan. *I ought to have thought of it before.* Waiting around for Mr. Smirch to get his crop in wasn't helping her pa at all. Suppose the judge had come back to town before Louisa got there? What if the trial had started already?

All the while her mind was running along these lines, her feet were carrying her away from the Smirch place. She'd been so intent on getting away before Mr. Smirch caught up to her that she hadn't paid much heed to where she was going; she'd just run. Now she realized that she was halfway to the hazel grove.

She stumbled to a stop, panting, listening for sounds behind her. Someone was calling out—a faint, faraway shout that she figured was her name. Mr. Smirch must be looking for her, but he wasn't anywhere close.

The grove might be a pretty good place to hide, she guessed, but she wasn't sure she dared to go there in the dark. The thought of encountering the—what was he?—gave her the shivers.

Then again, perhaps Jessamine was right; he seemed friendly enough. He'd retrieved Charlie's stone, and he'd gathered all those nuts for them.

Louisa hesitated, unsure of what to do.

Was it her imagination, or was Mr. Smirch's holler a little louder? All around her the tall grass rustled and whispered. Small skitterings and squeakings and cracklings rose up from the ground. Louisa shivered. She felt exposed, alone, foolish. Maybe she should just go on home after all and hide in the root cellar.

A howl rose up from the prairie, long and mournful and menacing, a terrible, hungry call, and from the sound of it, quite close by. Louisa's skin broke out in gooseflesh. She felt turned to stone by fear. That wolf could not be far off. And there she was, helpless as a fawn, right smack in the middle of open prairie.

That settled it: bearded fellow or not, she had to head for the grove. There were good-size cottonwoods there. Wolves couldn't climb trees.

She made herself take a step, and another. She dared not run—she hardly dared to breathe, lest the wolf, wherever it was, hear her and decide she sounded like a fine little dinner. She wished it would howl again, so at least she'd know where it was. The black air around her seemed alive with snuffling and soft, heavy tread. She could not hear Mr. Smirch anymore.

Step by step, she came closer to the grove. The dark, gnarled arms of the cottonwoods against the blue-black sky almost set her to crying, she was so relieved to see them. She couldn't help but hurry now; the trees beckoned with their stout branches. Every moment she expected to hear the dry grass snapping behind her under the weight of the wolf's terrible paws; every moment she expected to feel its hot breath on her neck. Sobbing, she ran to a tree, threw her arms around the trunk, and dug her heels in, scrambling and scraping her way up to the lowest branch. When she tried to swing her legs up and over the branch, her legs got caught in her skirt and petticoat, and frantically she flailed about, expecting the wolf's teeth to sink into her skin at any minute. Then suddenly she was up, clinging with all four limbs, her skirts torn and tangled around her. She peered down through the darkness, wondering if she was high enough, wondering how high a wolf could leap.

But she didn't see any wolf at all. To be sure, she could not see much of anything. But there were no evil eyes gleaming at her, no flashing teeth, no growl or snarl or scrabbling of paws at the tree trunk.

From somewhere not far away, but not right under the tree, the chilling howl curdled the air once more. Wherever the wolf was, it was not in the hazel grove.

Smarting with scrapes and bruises from her hasty ascent, her heart pounding, Louisa burst into tears, much to her own disgust. She lay there on the branch a minute, catching her breath, wishing this were all a bad dream and she was really home in her own bed, with Pa reading by lamplight in the next room.

But that line of thought threatened to bring back the tears.

"Stop it, Louisa," she told herself. "Don't be a goose."

"A goose indeed," said a voice from the darkness below. "I've not seen such a foolish spectacle as this since Farmer MacClellan came home late from the pub and set to paintin' his cottage with milk instead o' whitewash!"

CHAPTER FOURTEEN
What Sort of Fool

LOUISA SHRIEKED AND FELL OUT OF THE TREE.

She landed hard on her back and had the wind knocked out of her. Pinpoints of light glittered and swirled against her eyelids, and for a long moment she could neither hear nor speak. Then, slowly, the swirling light specks receded, and she found she could breathe again and open her eyes.

The little bearded man in the pointed cap was leaning over her, holding a tiny candle in a candlestick holder made from what looked like a hazelnut shell. His grizzled white beard was so long that the tip of it tickled Louisa's cheek. The little man's brows were drawn together in a disapproving frown.

"And that," he said in a funny, low voice that was rough and lilting at the same time, "was foolisher still."

"What—" Louisa gasped, at a loss for words. Her head was still spinning from the fall, and she ached all over. She stared up at the little man, trying to make sense of what was happening, but all that came to her mind were fragments of nonsense. *What a cunning little candle; Jessamine would go wild over it.*

"What indeed?" said the little man. "'Tis precisely the place to start. *What* are ye doin' in me grove? *What* made ye run like the banshee was on yer heels? And *what* ever possessed ye to drop like a stone out o' that poor tree and come crashin' down nearly on top o' me head?"

"S-sorry!" stammered Louisa, too flustered to consider the possibility that the person falling out of the tree stood more risk of injury than the person standing below. "I . . . I didn't know you were there."

"Obviously," said the little man drily. "I should hope ye wouldn't undertake to squash me on purpose."

"Oh, no!" Louisa assured him, sitting up. Pain swept through her head and she sank back, groaning.

"If that doesn't beat all," grumbled the little man. "Now ye've gone and hurt yerself, and I suppose next ye'll be wantin' me to play nursemaid." He held out a hand. "Come on, then. Upsy-daisy. Sooner ye're on yer feet, the sooner ye can go on yer way and leave me and me trees in peace."

Hesitantly, Louisa took hold of the small, gnarled hand. The little man's grip was surprisingly strong. His skin was dry and warm; grasping his hand was like grasping a sturdy tree branch.

He hauled her to her feet. Swaying, she clutched at the tree trunk to steady herself. Gradually the dizziness receded and she found she could stand alone. The little man stood regarding her with a sour expression on his funny, wrinkled face.

"Ye look like last year's scarecrow," he said. "Ye're not fit to take yerself back home, that's for certain."

"It isn't my home," said Louisa. "I can't go back there ever. They were going to cut my hair off."

The little man whistled. "Aye, that is bad. Cousin o' mine had his beard cut off once by some meddlesome lasses—exactly *yer* sort—and he was so shamed, he dared not show his face outside the hill for a hundred years."

Louisa blurted out the question before she stopped to think: "What—what *are* you, please?"

Shaggy brows drew together indignantly. "I might ask the same o' ye, pert miss," barked the little man. "What sort o' fool is it that goes traipsin' about the countryside in the dark under a wolf's moon?" He shrugged. "Same sort o' fool that falls out o' trees for no reason, I suppose."

"You startled me," explained Louisa. "I didn't know you were there."

"And here we go round this bush again," muttered the little man. "Mercy on me, I can see it's a long night I'm in for. Come, goose, I'll give ye summat to clear yer head, and then ye must skedaddle and stop pesterin' me. Twice in one day! At least ye left yer howlers at home this time."

"It isn't my home," repeated Louisa absently. It was all so puzzling, she could not think of anything else to say.

CHAPTER FIFTEEN
Ignore the Spiders

SHE FOLLOWED THE LITTLE MAN BETWEEN THE whispering trees. Their footsteps crackled on bits of leaf and hazelnut shell. Louisa found herself wondering if the little man wore shoes, but it was too dark to tell. His cap was a pointed darkness bobbing up and down before her. He led the way toward the hole beside the gray stone.

"Never a minute's peace," he grumbled, pausing before the hole. "I break me back gatherin' nuts to get rid o' the great lumberin' creatures—*my* nuts, I might add, which I can ill afford to spare—and what thanks do I get? Back one o' them comes the selfsame night, clawin' at me poor trees and disturbin' me rest!"

"You were only trying to get rid of us?" asked Louisa, astonished out of bashfulness. "We—Jessamine and I—thought you meant to be kind!"

The little man had turned to look at her, one shaggy eyebrow cocked impatiently. Now he snorted.

"Kind! Who thinks o' kindness when Big Folk are tramplin' yer winter's store? I knew ye'd only be back later to fill yer pail, and I thought it best to hasten ye on yer way as soon as possible. I might ha' known ye'd return to gawp at me later. A fine day it is, when an honest brownie canna be left in peace."

Harrumphing, he spun on his heel and stomped on. Louisa hurried to keep up with him.

"Please . . . what's a brownie?" she asked.

But the little man would not answer. Ignoring her, he stalked to his tunnel and gestured grimly for her to follow him inside.

"In there?" Louisa shrank away. "I . . . I couldn't!"

"Ye'll fit well enough if ye crawl," snapped the little man. "Just mind ye don't go bangin' yer great head on the roof and collapsin' me poor tunnel, which I dug with the sweat o' me own brow—and nary a hand did *she* lift to help me, I might say," he added in a mutter so low Louisa barely caught it. Briefly she wondered how the "brownie," as he'd called himself, could expect her to have helped dig a tunnel when she hadn't even known until today that such a thing as a brownie *existed*, much less needed help with excavation projects.

Her head still felt rattled from the fall—not to mention the terrifying flight from the wolf and the terrifying flight from Mrs. Smirch's scissors. She stood at the yawning black entrance, hesitant, befuddled. The brownie tapped his foot and beckoned impatiently.

"Are ye intendin' to stand there all night, ye great goose? 'Tis all the same to me if ye'd rather march yerself out o' me grove and leave me in blessed solitude once more. Just mind ye stay out o' me trees!"

Another wolf howl quivered in the distance. Louisa shuddered and dropped to her knees. She dared not think of what state her dress would be in come morning, what with climbing trees and falling out of trees and crawling down dark, mysterious tunnels in the middle of the night. *Mrs. Smirch will be furious,* she thought, and then she remembered she was never going back to that house. *Poor Jessamine.* The brownie gave her a slap on the back to get moving, as if she were a balky mule.

Blind as a mole, she fumbled her way along the underground path. Fearful thoughts of worms, snakes, and worse nibbled at the corners of her mind. Her head brushed the roof of the tunnel, causing bits of loose earth to rain down upon her back. The brownie, stalking along behind her, kept uttering his dark predictions of disaster; he seemed to take it as a given that any moment the whole tunnel was going to collapse on their heads. He seemed far more annoyed by the prospect of his hard work being undone than he was concerned about the apparently inconsequential perils of being buried alive.

"Keep on, keep on," he urged Louisa. "Can't ye go any faster?"

"I can't see anything!" she protested.

"There's naught to see," he said. "'Tis but me front passageway. Just keep straight on, and ignore the spiders. They talk overmuch, but they seldom bite."

CHAPTER SIXTEEN
The Underhill House

IT WAS JUST OCCURRING TO HER TO WONDER WHY the brownie had put her in front, since he was the one with the candle, and presumably he knew where they were going, when he snapped out a command to "Stop right there, and dinna ye move."

He scooted around her, the candle flickering ahead of him, and scuttled away around a curve, leaving Louisa alone in the dark. She was too shocked to be frightened at first, but before she had time to think, he was back, a bit breathless.

"Hurry up, then," he said, as if she'd been dawdling. She was beginning to think this strange little person was as disagreeable in his own way as Mrs. Smirch. Wearily she crawled after him, following him around the bend in the tunnel—and nearly colliding with him when he suddenly stopped short.

"Here we are," he said briskly. "Ye ought to be able to stand up now, if ye stoop a little. Why yer kind chooses to grow to such awkward heights is beyond me," he muttered as an afterthought as she rose unsteadily to her feet, ducking her head to keep from knocking it against the roof of the tunnel.

"We don't choose . . . ," began Louisa, but her retort died on her lips as she crossed the threshold from dark, bare earth to a setting altogether different. They seemed to be directly under one of the cottonwood trees, for great roots framed the floor and ceiling of what could only be described as a cozy little room. It was a small, snug, oblong space that reminded her of her father's dugout. It had the same whitewashed walls (though in the dugout, most of the whitewash had cracked and flaked away), and overhead there was a large piece of cloth spanning the ceiling. It appeared to be tacked to tree roots at either end of the room.

"To keep spiders from falling in the soup," Louisa murmured, remembering what Ma had said the day they moved into the new house. Dimly she could picture a cloth stretched similarly above the table in the old dugout. Standing here in the brownie's chamber, she had the strangest sense of being a very young child again—except in this dugout, her head nearly reached the cloth ceiling.

"Ye can sit here," said the brownie gruffly, indicating a chair made of polished wood and plump red cushions. "Ye're tall, but ye're not wide."

Gratefully Louisa lowered herself into the seat. She sank into the cushions, which were well stuffed with something soft and comfortable. The wood of the chair felt cool and smooth beneath her hands. A similar chair was drawn up opposite hers, that one upholstered in a lovely brown fabric that reminded her of a skirt her mother had worn.

"I'll fetch the tea," said the brownie. "Don't ye go touchin' anything." He glared at her in warning, then disappeared down a passageway Louisa had not noticed before. She wondered how many rooms he had down here and how far under the prairie his tunnels stretched.

Despite his surliness, the brownie seemed to keep quite a cozy home. The room was crowded with furniture and other objects: fat canvas sacks; small round barrels; flickering oil lamps on sleekly polished tables; and small woven baskets filled with nuts, potatoes, turnips, and carrots. Everything was lined up neatly against the

The effect was peculiar and pleasant;
it was like living in a patchwork quilt, Louisa thought.

walls, so that the open center of the room was occupied only by the two cushioned chairs with an empty round table between them.

Most of the walls were draped with fabric, just like the ceiling—long strips and squares of cloth in a variety of colors and patterns, each tacked to the tree roots that snaked along the walls. The effect was peculiar and pleasant; it was like living in a patchwork quilt, Louisa thought.

But who, she wondered, was the other chair for?

CHAPTER SEVENTEEN
Horseradish Tea

THE BROWNIE'S "TEA" WAS LIKE NOTHING LOUISA had ever tasted before. Her father had brought real tea leaves, dust-brown and brittle, home from trips to town once or twice a year, when he could get it. The Fletcher mercantile had trouble with its supply lines when the weather was particularly bad or the bandits particularly good. But the tea barrels came westward often enough that Louisa knew the sweet, aromatic bite of tea, and she knew at first sip that this sharp, throat-burning liquid was no relation to the beverage brewed from those crumbled leaves shipped all the way from India.

She tried to swallow politely, but it stung her throat and brought tears to her eyes.

"What ails ye? Don't ye care for horseradish?" demanded the brownie, bristling his brows in an offended manner.

"What's . . . horseradish?" Louisa gasped.

"There's no call for impertinence, lass," growled the brownie, his glare so hostile Louisa felt rather like she'd stumbled into a badger's den after all. "As if it didn't come from yer own larder."

"What do you mean?" Louisa asked, more sharply than she intended. Her mouth was still on fire. The brownie gave a guilty start and turned hastily away, sloshing "tea" out of the cup.

"Impertinence," he repeated, but all the quivering indignation had gone out of him. He would not meet Louisa's gaze, but instead stood staring at the dark splotch of liquid soaking into the earthen floor. "Bother," he muttered, and then startled Louisa with a sudden shout. "DON'T COME UP! YE WON'T LIKE IT!"

Louisa gaped, completely bewildered. The whole evening was beginning to seem like a dream, only more outlandish. Now the brownie was stomping and jumping, pounding his feet hard on the floor.

"I SAID DINNA BOTHER COMIN' UP! 'TIS NO FOR THE LIKES O' YE!"

"I'm sorry," said Louisa, "but I don't have the faint-est idea what you mean."

"I'm no speakin' to ye," said the brownie. "It's the blasted worms. They *will* come up for every wee drop o' water, and horseradish tea gives them gout."

For a long moment Louisa said nothing. She sat in the plush red chair, her nose and throat still stinging from the terrible tea, and watched as the brownie con-tinued to stamp and dance and bark his warnings to the worms. One hapless worm actually did break through the damp earth, rearing up and swaying from side to side in a manner Louisa had never witnessed in a worm before, his movements so agitated that it really did seem as though he were scolding the brownie.

"Ye've only yerself to blame!" barked the brownie in reply. "Only a fool drinks first and asks questions afterward." He gave a last stomp, and the worm hastily retreated into the earthen floor.

"I thought," ventured Louisa at last, "that gout was to do with *feet*."

The brownie snorted. "For them as *has* feet. A worm's whole body may as well be his foot, so ye can see why they get so cross."

A clock chimed. Louisa began counting automati-cally, but by the fifth bell it struck her that she *knew* that chime—knew it in the beat of her heart, the rhythm of her breath. She had marked her hours by that clear-toned bell-song as long as she could remember; she had lain in bed at night counting nine bongs and knowing Pa would be banking the hearthfire and pulling in the latchstring on the front door. The chiming was coming from the opposite side of the room, but even as she turned to search for its source, the brownie was scurrying across the room toward it. She watched in astonishment as he snatched at one of the cloths tacked to the earthen wall and flung it, dirty as it was, over what could only have been the clock.

Her clock—hers and Pa's. Louisa was certain of it.

"Balderdash!" cried the brownie, as if Louisa had spoken her accusation aloud.

"I didn't say anything!"

"What? O' course ye did. Impertinent, that's what ye are!"

"But really," protested Louisa, "I didn't say a word!"

"Oh, a *word*, is it," sneered the little man. "As if words are the only things you Big Folk use to *say* with. Ye with yer humphings and yer sighings and yer everlastin' gaspings! I never heard the like o' humans for gaspin'. Ye're the only creatures under heaven that do it, ye know. I don't mind tellin' ye the rest of us find it quite annoyin'."

Louisa drew in an indignant breath and then choked on it, realizing it might be considered a gasp. She had risen to her feet in search of the clock, but now she flopped back down in the red-cushioned chair, completely exasperated.

"I know that's our clock you're hiding," she said. "Pa's and mine. I suppose you took the rest of it too. *You're* the reason my pa got thrown in jail."

The brownie said nothing. He had set the pewter teacup down while he was shouting at the worm, and now he picked it up and absently drank from it, a furrow-browed sip, then the whole cup, tipping back his head to get the dregs. Louisa wondered how his hat did not fall off. He smacked his lips and, banging the cup down hard upon a little side table made of a tree stump, became suddenly very busy wiping his bristling beard and mustache.

"That's my eggcup!" cried Louisa. She had not recognized it at first because everything was so strange in this strangest of all dwellings, but now that she saw it on the table, she knew it for what it was. She had thought it odd that the brownie's teacups had squatty stems instead of handles, but filled with liquid (even nasty horseradish brew), it looked rather like a goblet, only very small. Now she saw that it was one of the four little pewter eggcups from her mother's sideboard. Most days

Louisa scrambled three or four eggs for breakfast, or else she fried them in the big cast-iron frypan. Pa liked them hard-boiled, too, especially during a plow time or harvest when he had to work from sunup to sundown; Louisa would carry his dinner out to the fields in a tin pail or basket, tucked under a bright napkin. But once in a while, on a Sunday, Pa would make soft-boiled eggs for breakfast and serve them in eggcups. It always made Louisa giggle to see him tapping daintily on the shell with his spoon, prinking his little finger for a joke.

All of a sudden Louisa was boiling mad. Up till now she had felt too muddled to take it all in properly; the dizzying events of this strange evening had unfolded too rapidly, been altogether too much. Head lice—scissors—wolves—brownie—tunnel—spiders—gouty earthworms—stolen clocks—too much! But now, faced with the pewter eggcup, a thing so familiar she could almost see Pa's face above it, she felt a rush of fury.

"You're the reason my pa got thrown in jail!" she repeated. "How dare you! How dare you take our things!"

"Ye'd better mind yer tone, Miss Impertinence," snapped the brownie. "'Tisn't I who made the laws bindin' Folk Big and Wee. I've tradition on my side goin' back two thousand years. Ye're lucky I didn't do worse than borrow a few old things ye didn't never use nohow.

'Twas within me rights to curdle yer cow's milk and stop yer hens from layin', and worse than that, for what ye done to me!"

"Whatever did we do to you?" asked Louisa, utterly mystified.

The brownie snorted. "Humph! What *didn't* ye do is more the tune of it. All these years I've worked for ye, savin' yer chicks from the hawks and yer wheat from the blight, and not once since yer mother died has anyone left me a drop o' cream in a saucer, though saucers ye have aplenty!"

"Do you mean you've been helping us all these years? Did you really watch over our chicks?"

"Did a great deal more than that, I did, as sure as me name is Angus MacClellan Brody O'Gorsebush."

"Brody? That's my name! I'm Louisa Brody."

"Dinna ye think I know that?" barked the brownie. "Where do you think me name comes from? We brownies always take the name of the Big Folk we help. 'Twas the MacClellans afore you, in the Auld Country."

"You were helping us," said Louisa slowly. "I . . . I didn't know. Nor did Pa; he'd have told me. He'd have wanted to thank you. My pa always pays his debts."

"Harrumph," said the brownie, looking uncomfortable. "'Tisn't a matter of *debt*. It's Tradition. Since time out o' mind, brownies have been lookin' after things on Big Folks' farms, and the Big Folks show their appreciation by leavin' us a bite to eat." He glowered at her, but there was something softer in his glare. "I do love a nice smack o' cream."

"People can't show appreciation if they don't know you exist," said Louisa. "I never heard of brownies before."

"Never . . . heard of . . . brownies!" sputtered the little man. "That what comes o' livin' in the middle o' blasted nowhere! No proper bringin'-up, that's what. No auld grannies to tell ye the way o' things. Why, we've been lookin' after the Big Folk in Scotland for time out o' mind. Centuries upon centuries." He grumbled into his eggcup and took a sip of his tea. "Yer mother'd ha' taught ye, I'll warrant, had she lived. She may ha' been Irish, but she was a fast learner, she was."

"Wait," gasped Louisa. "Do you mean my mother knew about you?"

"Whisht!" interrupted the brownie, holding up a hand. "D'ye hear that?"

For the second time that day someone leaned close, peering at Louisa's head with scrutinizing eyes. She was about to burst out in an exasperated protest—if she did have head lice, it had to be entirely the fault of that dirty, lumpy straw tick she'd been forced to sleep on at the Smirches' house—but before she could speak, the brownie began to whisper.

"Hush-a-marra, wee ones," he murmured. "I'm sure 'tis clean and cozy there, but ye've no call to go bitin' a poor bonny lass. Off wi' ye, now. There's a coyote den just down the river a bit—plenty o' nice eatin' for the likes o' ye."

Louisa's scalp began to itch. She raised a hand automatically, but the brownie stilled her.

"Just ye bide a moment. 'Twill tickle, but they mean no harm."

It was the creepiest feeling Louisa had ever felt. Something—*things*—were walking across her head, down her neck—she shuddered, longing to slap and scratch them away—across the shoulders of her dirt-stained dress, down her back, and down to the floor. Mrs. Smirch had been right: she had head lice. And now?

Now they were leaving because the brownie had asked them to.

CHAPTER EIGHTEEN
Spilling Over with Secrets

THE STRANGEST DAY OF LOUISA'S LIFE SO FAR ended more strangely than the strangest thing she could ever have imagined. The brownie showed her to a small rounded chamber that opened off the main room where he had served her the atrocious horseradish tea. In the dim light she had not seen that one part of the living-room wall rose only partway to the cloth-covered earthen ceiling. There was a small alcove above the wall, framed partly by tree roots and partly by large flat slabs of stone. The brownie had climbed up first by way of a small wooden ladder and rummaged around out of sight for a few minutes, his feet in their soft red boots still tiptoed on the bottom rung—preparing her bed, he explained.

Then he had backed down the ladder and spent some time in considerable consternation at the realization that Louisa was far too big for the ladder, which seemed to be made of tree branches bound together with ropes of braided grass. At last he settled upon a solution that involved hauling the tea table over to the wall beside the ladder, from which Louisa was able to reach the lip of the alcove and pull herself, to the peril of her dress, into the little shelflike room. There was indeed a fine bed awaiting her there, comprised of a length of fabric spread over a soft, heaping pile of reasonably clean carded wool. Mrs. Smirch, she recalled, had complained of losing a sack of wool, and Louisa could not help but take some satisfaction in the suspicion that this was that stolen fleece. Then she recognized the bedsheet as one of her own parlor curtains, and did not know whether to scream or laugh.

The alcove was wide enough, but not nearly long enough, for a tall human girl. She lay with her legs curled, her toes right at the edge of the chamber, listening to the soft noise of the brownie padding around in the living room below. She wondered how many rooms he had here under the hazel grove. Surely there could not be much more to this cavern space above the riverbank, or else he would have put her in a proper room instead

There was a small alcove above the wall, framed partly by tree roots and partly by large flat slabs of stone.

of this lumpy rock-ledge where the tree roots caught at her hair when she rolled over. There was precious little room for rolling, anyway.

She tried not to think about the weight of the earth above her or the creeping things in the crannies all around. At least it was not pitch-dark, as one might expect an underground chamber to be in the dead of night. There was a glow of dim light coming from somewhere, a pale, white light, but no matter how she craned her neck around to search, she could not tell where it came from.

She awoke in panic and pain, having banged her head on a rock or a root or possibly both in her sleep. The light was just as pale and dim as it had been when she drifted off. She could not tell whether it was morning yet; she only knew that she was cold and hungry and needed most urgently to find a privy, or some reasonable substitute. She hoped the brownie would not expect her to use a chamber pot. She would rather slip away to the creek alone. And then she would find him and thank him for the night's lodging, and figure out how to get herself the thirteen miles into town to clear her father's name before the circuit judge returned and had him hung.

First things first, she told herself, struggling to

combat the towering fear that rose up within her at the thought of her father's dangerous situation. *A privy.*

She began to back out of the alcove, her feet jutting out into empty air. She hoped the brownie had left the tea table in place below the opening.

"Hello!" she called. "Mr. O'Gorsebush, sir? I'm coming down, please."

Her feet scrabbled for the table. She was holding herself on the ledge by her elbows, her face smushed against the cold rock shelf. One foot found a surface down below. Gingerly, she put weight on it. The brownie let out a yelp, and the surface moved out from under her foot.

"What d'ye think ye're about?" cried the brownie. "Steppin' bang on me head. And me wi' me nightcap on! Is it a ladder ye think I be?"

Louisa had to stay there hanging by her elbows, her legs dangling down, until the brownie dragged the tree-stump tea table underneath her feet, grumbling all the while. Really, she thought, he was as disagreeable in his way as Mrs. Smirch was in hers—and a thief to boot. Although the brownie had helped her last night—saved her life, even—Louisa could not forget that it was his fault she was in this scrape to begin with. He had taken things from her house and Mr. Smirch's. He had, for reasons Louisa could not begin to fathom, stored the stolen goods in her father's old dugout. He had done nothing when the sheriff came and carted her father away. And what good would it do now for Louisa to explain, even if she could hike thirteen miles to town in time to save her father? Who would believe her when she explained about the brownie?

After all, she herself had not believed Jessamine's account of seeing a strange little man in a pointy brown cap.

The cap, as far as Louisa could tell, seemed to be the brownie's prized possession. He had hastened out of the room while Louisa climbed down from the tea table, barking out to her not to turn around until he said it was all right. He appeared in mortal dread of being seen without his brown cap.

Perhaps, Louisa thought, his head was as pointy as the cap.

The tunnel-house was not much brighter in the daytime than it was at night. At least, Louisa assumed it was morning; she was hungry enough that it might well be noon. She ached to be in her own home, where she could have fresh clothes, a bath in the big tin tub, a nice plate of cornbread with molasses, some of Evangeline's good, fresh milk. Maybe she *could* sneak over for a little while, she mused. After all, the Smirches might look for her there, but they could hardly spare a whole day's work—though Louisa wouldn't put it past Mrs. Smirch to plant Winthrop and Charlie on her doorstep as lookouts. Well, they would never stay put without Jessamine to keep watch over them, and Jessamine, Louisa knew, would help her. She'd think up some excuse to distract the boys away from the house, for sure.

The musing began to crystallize into a plan. One way or another, Louisa would need some supplies before she could begin the long hike to town. Exactly what she'd do when she got there was another matter altogether; she'd ford that creek when she came to it.

She supposed Jessamine must be worried sick about her, out all night on her own. Louisa began to hope Jessamine *would* be on boy-minding duty at her place. If not, she ought to think of a way to leave a message for the little girl somehow, so she wouldn't worry too much.

But how?

The brownie erupted from his tunnel into the living room, beard combed and brown cap brushed clean of the dirt and cobwebs that had adorned its peak last night.

"What? Not washed up yet? Och, I never saw the like o' humans for lollygaggin' and malingerin'. There isn't another creature under heaven that stands around woolgatherin' when there's work to be done."

Louisa tried to protest—it was not as if her host had shown where to find so much as a water basin, after all—but the brownie paid her no mind. He opened the front door and then turned back to shout something at the worms, and he stopped in the tunnel to have a long conversation with a dung beetle, all while Louisa crouched behind him feeling rather desperate. If she didn't get to a privy soon—or the far side of a tree, or *something*—she feared she was going to have an accident. At her age! The thought was beyond mortifying. She didn't want to know what the earthworms would have to say about *that*.

But at last the brownie finished his long-winded tunnel business and led the way down the dim corridor, emerging slowly into the sunlight after much careful listening and peering about. Louisa didn't blame him for being wary. If Charlie and Winthrop ever caught wind of him, he'd never again know a moment's peace.

He had dawdled so long that Louisa had no time for niceties. "I beg your pardon!" she gasped and dashed into the hazel grove, hiding herself where the bushes were thickest. Perhaps the brownie had sense enough to guess what she was up to, for he struck up a rather loud conversation with some creature Louisa could not see. The replies seemed to be of a *hoo*ing and *ooh*ing sort, so she supposed he was speaking to an owl in one of the treetops. She hoped the owl could not see her makeshift privy.

Her face was burning with embarrassment when she rejoined the brownie at the mouth of his tunnel. He took no notice of her, but went on hollering to the owl—a great horned owl, she saw now, peering up over the edge of a messy stick nest half-hidden by the leaves of the tallest cottonwood. It turned its large placid gaze upon her, blinking slowly, the bottom eyelids coming up to meet the top. A tuft of feather stuck up on either side of its head like ears. It clicked its beak, blinked again, and turned its head back toward the brownie.

"Hoowoo," it said.

"I'm well aware of that," said the brownie impatiently. "Just see that ye leave the chicks be, and pass the word to the other flyers. I suppose I'll have to speak to the snakes meself. Sure and I shudder to think what *she'll* have to say about that."

Louisa wondered what on earth he was talking about. What she'd have to say about what? His speaking to snakes? It sounded rather interesting—quite a useful talent, in her opinion.

"Come on, then!" the brownie cried, startling her. He switched so abruptly from one thing to another. "We've got to hurry! Ought to ha' been there half an hour ago!"

"Been *where?*" demanded Louisa in exasperation. "You don't . . . I haven't . . . oh please, I have to go home! I have to go into town to help my father, and I'll need some things to help me get there, you see."

She spoke in a rush, hoping to get the words out before the brownie hustled her off on some inscrutable brownie errand. He gave her a pop-eyed stare and pulled impatiently on his beard with both fists so that it wound up in two long neat points.

"'Go home,' she says," he fumed. "Where in thunder d'ye think we're goin', lass! To see to things at yer place before that sour-faced, thatch-headed giant arrives and steals all me nice warm milk away."

"Oh!"

Louisa hurried after him through the ring of trees toward the open plain. At the edge of the grove he veered east, skirting the Smirches' land, following the curve of one of the low hills that undulated out from the creek bottoms. Louisa had never been here before, as far as she recalled. She thought of the view from her front porch at home, the broad flat plain that wasn't really flat at all, but rather a vast expanse of land full of billows and wrinkles and flat places, like a bedsheet waiting to be smoothed. This hill must be, she realized, one of those billows in the sheet.

That view of the broad billowing sheet, white as goosedown in winter, its ripples softened and blunted, or golden brown in the middle of a baking hot summer; or blue-green in the spring, sprigged with red and orange like calico—oh how she loved that view, loved to stand on her porch with Pa after supper, watching the sun sink, pouring its color into the sky and the clouds and the golden ribbon of the horizon. Pa would point out a flash of white, then another, and another, that meant a family of pronghorn antelope were streaking white-rumped across the prairie like low comets. A turkey vulture circling, circling, its huge wings tipped with broad feathers set wide apart so that they looked like fingers trailing in the sky. A ripple in the grasses, fat seedheads bending and quivering, where some small creature was trotting unseen—a fox, perhaps, or a jackrabbit, a coyote, a badger.

"This land is spillin' over with secrets, Louisa," Pa would say. "If we had eyes like one o' them eagles up there, we might could read some o' them."

The brownie was moving forward between the tall grasses so rapidly that Louisa could hardly see anything of him but the tip of his hat. She quickened her pace, aching to stand on her own porch again, staring out at this view that held so many more secrets than she had ever imagined. *I'm one of them now myself,* she thought.

CHAPTER NINETEEN

A Very Good Question

THEY CREPT CAUTIOUSLY THROUGH THE CORNFIELD toward the barn, keeping a wary eye out for signs of Mr. Smirch. Close to the barn's back wall, the brownie cocked his eye and held up a hand in warning. He seemed to be listening. Louisa held her breath, trying to hear what he was hearing.

"By the kelpie's mane!" the brownie burst out. "He's taken the cow, blast him."

"Evangeline?" Louisa hurried around the corner of the barn behind the little man.

"Evangeline," snorted the brownie, coming to a halt in the wide doorway. "Is that what ye call her?"

The barn doors had been left open, and the cow was

gone. At first Louisa thought, with considerable alarm, that Mr. Smirch must have been careless enough to leave the doors open after he milked the evening before, allowing Evangeline to wander off—or worse, wolves to wander *in*. But the deserted stall showed no signs of unpleasantness, and a hasty conversation between the brownie and a meadowlark revealed that Mr. Smirch had returned to the farm in the dark the night before and gone all over the house with a lantern, hollering and clomping, making it altogether impossible for the lark to settle down for the night. After seventeen choruses of this unmelodic song (so the meadowlark explained), the man had clomped back to the barn and led the cow away.

"He must have been looking for me," said Louisa, feeling a bit guilty that Mr. Smirch had had to hike the two miles over here and back twice in one evening, for he had scarcely returned from milking Evangeline an hour before his wife had insisted Louisa read to the family after supper. "I suppose he didn't want to have to come back first thing this morning for another milking. He must have taken her to his own barn."

"Impertinence!" said the brownie. "First the milk, and now the cow. I don't suppose he asked *her* if she wanted to go traipsin' off into the dark. And her so terrible afraid o' the moon."

"She is?" asked Louisa, but he had gone off, muttering in disgust, to tend to the chickens.

The brownie did not seem to want her help, so she went to the well and filled a pail with water for a wash. She longed to change her clothes, but her other work dress was at the Smirches', and she wanted to keep her Sunday frock clean for when she got to town.

Town. It was thirteen miles away—farther than she had ever walked in her life. Her toes wiggled inside her tight boots. Pa had said he'd buy her a new pair of shoes after the wheat was sold. She added a pair of stockings to the small pile she was assembling for her pack: a sunbonnet, a wedge of cheese, a jug of water, some wrinkled ropes of venison jerky she and Pa had made the previous winter. She tied the pile up in a bedsheet. It was clumsy, but it would have to do.

The house looked dusty, neglected, lonely. Louisa ached to fly around with broom and dustcloth and make it look neat and lived-in again. Instead she took Pa's comb and a basin of water and combed out her tangled hair, then braided it into two long plaits. She checked the comb anxiously for signs of yesterday's unwelcome visitors and found nothing. *That's a mercy, at least,* she thought.

She found the brownie in the barnyard outside the chicken coop, conversing with the brown hen.

"Don't get yerself in a bother," he said. "The bull snakes and the hognose snake have been warned. I'll stop up their hidey-holes with cow dung if they so much as flick a tongue in yer direction. Mind, I've not found anyone willin' to convey me message to that infernal rattler. Foul-tempered creature, he is; we don't tolerate that kind o' nasty temper in the Auld Country. But there's no need to go rufflin' up yer feathers worriting over *him*. Meadowlark says he gorged on a prairie dog and is too stuffed to move. 'Twill be the better part of a week before he's back on the prowl. And the winged poachers have promised to mind their manners."

The brown hen clucked and danced and fluttered her wings, and behind her a line of yellow chicks gave a simultaneous cheep. The brownie nodded in approval. "That's the spirit, missus. 'Tis a fine handsome brood ye're raisin', and mannerly as well."

Louisa nearly clapped in delight. "Can you talk to everything?" she asked. "Birds and snakes and mice and everything?"

"Mice! I'm glad ye reminded me. I must have a word with the field mice—I'll not have them invadin' yer pantry while ye're away."

"Will they obey you?"

The brownie snorted. "Obey me! Mice obey no

master. Clever things, they are, however, and this lot are grateful ye keep no cats around. They'll listen to reason. I'll point out they don't want ye bringin' home any kittens from town."

Town. Involuntarily Louisa gazed westward, following the trail of trees that marked the path of Spitwhistle Creek. She could see a long way across the prairie, but town was too far away even to glimpse.

"I ought to get started," she said. "How long do you suppose it takes to walk thirteen miles?"

"Walk—" the brownie began, but a sudden shrill whistle from the mockingbird halted his words. The chicks peep-peeped in alarm, running to shelter under their mother's wings. Someone was coming. Louisa's impulse was to hide in the henhouse, but before she could move, a body came hurtling around the corner of the barn.

It was Jessamine, hair unkempt, feet bare, breathing hard.

"Louisa!" she cried, throwing her arms around the older girl. "Oh good, I was so afraid you'd be hidin' somewhere," she panted, letting go of the bear hug and leaning over with her hands on her knees, trying to catch her breath, "and I didn't know where to look . . . I tried the hazel grove first because my uncle had already searched here and said you were nowhere to be found, and I looked in all the trees and you weren't there, and I was going to look in the tunnel just in case, but—can you imagine!—a big old owl swooped at my head and wouldn't let me go near it! Did you ever hear of such a thi—"

She broke off abruptly, staring with wide, unbelieving eyes at the brownie. He stood beside Louisa with his hands on his hips, scowling.

"You!" Jessamine gasped. "It's you! I knew you weren't a badger!"

"A badger!" snapped the brownie. "Ridiculous. Hmph. So I see it's *ye* I have to thank for mixin' me up in this business. This *human* business," he added darkly.

Jessamine's brow furrowed anxiously. "I . . . I did? I didn't mean—"

Louisa interrupted her. "Don't mind Mr. O'Gorsebush, Jessamine. You didn't do anything wrong. Your aunt is the one who sent us to the hazel grove. I only ran there last night because I was afraid of wolves and thought I'd be safer in a tree." She turned to the brownie, whom she was beginning to realize was a great deal more bark than bite. "And besides, *you're* the one who got *us* mixed up in this business, remember? If you hadn't hidden all those things in my pa's dugout, he wouldn't be sitting in jail right now!"

The brownie harrumphed and—in a rather astonishing display of rudeness, Louisa thought, even for him—turned his back on her.

"You're the thief?" shrilled Jessamine. "You took my aunt's doll? And my uncle's hatchet? And the clock and everything? Whatever for?"

"That's a very good question," said Louisa, marching around the brownie until she faced him again. "You haven't explained that part at all. I understand you were sore about our not being grateful for all the help you've given us. And now that I know, I *am* grateful, ever so much! But why did you put all those things in our old dugout? Why didn't you take them to your, um, house, like our clock and my eggcup and the other things? Were you trying to get my pa in trouble?"

"Now why in thunder would I want to do that?" exploded the brownie. "It's cost me a world o' trouble, him bein' arrested."

"Then *why*?"

The brownie murmured something too soft for Louisa to hear.

"Beg pardon?"

"For her! 'Twas all for her, d'ye understand?"

"Who?" asked the girls in unison.

The brownie, his face turning tomato-red with emotion, grabbed handfuls of his beard with both fists and tugged with a rather alarming intensity.

"Who d'ye think, ye great, green, giddy, gallumpin' geese! My *wife*!"

CHAPTER TWENTY

In the Dugout

"YOUR WIFE?" LOUISA GASPED.

The brownie's beard was quivering in two pointed chunks, his nose and cheeks quite purple above the snowy forks of it. He strode across the barnyard, beetle-browed, arms crossed over his rounded middle. The brown hen's chicks chased after him in a stumbling, fluffy line, peeping frantically. Jessamine and Louisa exchanged baffled glances.

"Well," called the brownie over his shoulder, having stopped suddenly, which caused the line of chicks to collapse in on itself and then erupt in a fresh frenzy of peeping. "Are ye comin' or are ye not?"

By now Louisa knew better than to ask, *Coming*

where? Taking Jessamine by the hand, she followed the brownie out of the barnyard and up the path toward her father's old dugout.

The door stuck. Louisa had to yank it hard before it swung open, knocking her off balance and causing another chain reaction among the chicks, who were sticking close behind the brownie. He was still scowling, as if someone had done him wrong and not the other way around. Jessamine, on the other hand, was eager-eyed and red-cheeked, as if she were going to a party where there might be lemonade or even ice cream.

It was dark in the room cut into the hillside, darker even than the brownie's house had been. Louisa remembered the shafts of sunlight filtering down through the knot of tree roots overhead; she supposed the brownie had worked out some kind of skylight system for ventilation and light. The dugout had had a window-hole next to the door once, covered over with oiled paper, but in the long years of its disuse, the buffalo grass of the hillside had put out runners across the small opening.

With the door open at its widest, there was a long plank of sunlight laid on the floor, above which swirled a dim galaxy of dust motes. Louisa stepped into the dugout, swallowing past the burning in her throat. The last time she'd been here was that day with Mr. Smirch and the hatchet, her last full day with Pa.

Jessamine had slipped inside and was spinning slowly round, like the dust motes, exploring the room with her eyes.

"It's a home," she said. She turned to the brownie. "You were going to live here. With your wife."

The brownie scowled harder, staring at the ground. Around his boots, the chicks eddied and peeped.

Louisa saw now what she had not noticed that day with Mr. Smirch. She had seen the things he named with such fury: his hatchet, his clock, his wife's doll. She had not seen that the dugout was not the dusty bare shed it had been for most of her lifetime. It was a *room*, half-furnished and lovingly decorated. It lacked a bed, table, chairs—things the brownie must have been planning to move from the tunnel-house after he'd sprung the surprise on his wife. But there were wooden shelves mounted on the wall, carefully arranged with objects: a canning jar filled with buttons, an eggbeater, a tin cup. Her mother's tortoiseshell comb. There were spaces where the Smirches' clock and doll had been.

"You were setting up housekeeping!" she said to the brownie.

Jessamine clapped her hands. "It's lovely, what you've done."

The brownie's frown was carved so deep he looked made of stone. He bent and lowered a hand, palm outstretched, and one of the chicks clambered on, peeping ecstatically. Silently, he stroked its small fluffy head with one gnarled finger.

Louisa saw that he'd tacked a cloth into the earthen ceiling overhead here, just as he had in the tunnel-house. Her throat burned; she could remember standing in this very spot, staring upward at the checked oilcloth, hearing Mama hum behind her at the squatty iron cookstove. The stove was in the frame house now; Louisa had cooked hundreds of meals on it. She turned around to look at the empty space where it had lived when she was little, following the path of the absent stovepipe up to the low ceiling. The stovepipe hole had long since disappeared under the thick mat of grass above.

The brownie spoke at last. "Wanted a proper house, me wife did," he muttered. "Our folk have lived underground for time out o' mind, but that was in the Auld Country, where we had neighbors aplenty. Not just the wild creatures—the weasels and owls and hares—but our own kind. Brownies, dryads, boggarts—nasty-tempered folk they are, but they kept things lively-like. There was a kelpie in the pool down the way, and betimes we rode owlback to the seashore to visit with me wife's cousins— she's got a trace o' selkie blood, and I suppose that's where the trouble came from. Selkies never could keep content wi' their own lot. Always wantin' to shed their sealskins and go mingle with the Big Folk, and gettin' themselves stuck there and pinin' away after the sea." He gave a great sigh, staring down at the yellow chick. "Pinin' away herself, she was. Me grand wife. Pinin' away, and 'twas all my doin', fool that I am!"

"How?" whispered Jessamine.

"Our Big Folk were leavin', y'see. Packin' their things in crates and chatterin' about America this and America that. Our kind had tended their barns for hundreds o' years, but now they were leavin' with nary a thought for us. No more nice bowls o' cream to thank ye for a night's work. No more bowls o' porridge. They sold off the livestock—our friends, weren't they, that we loved like our own bairns? I still mind the day the cow was marched away down the road, bawlin' her poor heart out. And me wife, cryin' into her apron like a selkie who'd lost its skin. Och, those were dark days."

Louisa blinked away the tears that had come to her eyes. The brownie's gruff voice was so soft, so mournful.

"At last," he continued, "I decided we ought to go

wi' them. Our Big Folk. Come to this America they were always goin' on about. 'Twas the foolishest notion ever a brownie had in all o' history. We nearly died on the sea voyage—no ventilation at all in the crate we were hidin' in, and if the ship rats hadn't gnawed us free, we'd have perished for sure. And then the weeks in Boston—wagons everywhere, and boots, and noise. And the worst blow came when our Big Folk decided not to farm anymore. Took factory jobs, they did, and rented squalid rooms in a tenement. No air, no stars. No creatures to care for. Mice and rats don't need help from the likes of us, do they?"

He gently placed the chick back upon the ground. It skittered to its mother's side, and the other chicks crowded in close around it, cheeping wildly. The brownie watched them absently, stroking his beard back into one point.

"Took a toll on the missus, it did. Neither one of us felt like we could get a proper breath of air. In the end, we left our Big Folk—them as we'd looked after for time out o' mind. 'Twas terrible hard, but what could we do? They'd forgotten us, anyway. One day in the public square—we used to go sometimes, to visit some geese with whom we'd become acquainted—we heard a young man tellin' a shopkeeper he and his bride were fixin' to go west, to 'carve a little farm out o' the wilderness,' he said. Well, I liked the sound o' that. A young family, just startin' out. There'd be a world o' work to be done, plenty to keep a brownie busy. And he was a fine upstandin' young man, I could see that. To be sure, he was an Irishman, and me a Scot. Och! But we could see he was mannerly and hardworkin', with a spring in his step and a thatch o' red hair that'd make anyone proud."

"My pa!" cried Louisa.

"Aye. Your pa. And your ma, a sprightly thing she was. My wife took a shine to her right off. And so we decided to go west wi' them. We crept into their wagon, and when they stopped and commenced makin' a new life, so did we. Here we've been ever since."

"Did they know you were in their wagon?" asked Jessamine.

"Of course not. What do you take me for, a leprechaun? A brownie never shows his face to a Big Person." He scowled. "I've no business standin' here talkin' to ye now."

"But," said Louisa, "where is your wife?"

The brownie's scowl deepened.

"She was never happy here," he muttered. "There aren't any of our sort to be found. Not so much as a boggart. Our first year, me missus was that lonely, she near went off her head, poor lass. Och, sure and she tried to make friends, but the creatures here were distrustful at first. They'd never seen our like. Why, that first summer we were nearly gobbled up by an eagle, three snakes, and an owl! Impertinence. We soon set them straight. The mice and voles came around after we planted the hazel-nuts we'd brought with us from the Auld Country and raised up that fine grove. And there was a crow who was quite neighborly. But it took longer for the pronghorn to trust us, and the mule deer.

"And all the while, me wife was pinin' for some real conversation, she said. 'All the prairie creatures want to chat about is eatin' and avoidin' being eaten,' she'd complain. I tried to tell her she needed to give it time. The owls in particular have quite a lot to say, once they overcome their reticence. And yer father's cow is as fine a storyteller as I've ever had the pleasure o' listenin' to. She can tell a ghost tale 'twould make your hair fall out."

"Evangeline?" said Louisa in surprise. "Oh, I wish I could hear her!"

"Ye can hear well enough, ye just can't understand," said the brownie tartly.

"But what happened to your wife?" asked Jessamine anxiously. "The snakes didn't get her, did they?"

"Och, nay, naught o' the sort. But she sank into a

great woe, she did. All the spark went out o' her. She threatened to leave—said she'd had it up to here with the loneliness and the wailin' wind, and the Big Folk never leavin' out so much as a thimbleful o' milk—"

"You mean my parents! But they didn't know you were there!" interrupted Louisa.

"Whisht! Never you mind, child. Likely 'twouldn't have mattered anyway. 'Twas plain homesickness that ailed her as much as anythin'. No kelpie in the pond, no pixies under the trees. No sea to call to her selkie blood. And the mean, cramped quarters there under the roots. Ye've seen them. Ye know. She said it was one thing to live underground back in the Auld Country, where 'tis so crowded, every nook and cranny home to some creature or other. But out here, in this wide-rollin' land, she felt alone under the moon, she said. Alone under the moon. Wastin' away, she was, and I thought for a time she might fade altogether.

"But she perked right up after she met yer mother."

"What?" Louisa gasped. *"My mother?"*

"Aye. She spied me, she did, for hadn't I ventured out o' cover to chase a fox away from the chicken yard?"

The brown hen clucked appreciatively.

"Ye're most welcome, ma'am. Your great-great-great-great-great-grandmother, 'twas, and a fine bonny hen she was too. The fox was nigh upon her when I caught up to him. Grabbed his great bushy tail, I did, and gave it such a yank, he wound up an inch longer afterward. Och, he was that furious, I thought he'd gobble me up—him not havin' learned yet the proper way o' things twixt beasts and brownies. I gave him a right talkin' to, and off he skulks, tail draggin'. And I turned around and there was yer ma, watchin' the whole blessed thing. Standin' in this very doorway, she was, a pan o' dishwater in her hands and her mouth wide open. 'Course I ran for cover, but I knew it was too late. 'We're spied,' says I to me wife, and sure if her eyes didn't light up. She was glad, she was! 'I'm goin' right over there and make friends with her,' says she. 'Why, ye mustn't, mistress!' says I. 'That's nae the way things are done and ye know it.' 'What care I,' scoffs she, 'for the way things are done in the Auld Country. 'Tis a new world here, and new rules. I've liked the looks o' that lass from the start, and I'm after intendin' to befriend her.'

"Well, I roared and raged, but 'twas no use. She trips over here, pretty as you please, and next thing ye know, she's sittin' in this very room, drinkin' coffee out o' that there tin cup." He pointed at the shelf, his scowl reappearing. "Coffee, I ask you!"

"My ma knew about you," said Louisa. "All that time. Did my pa know?"

"Nay, my missus hadn't thrown every last scrap o' caution to the wind. She told yer mother that if ever she whispered to a soul about us, we'd disappear like thistledown in a gale and she'd never see us again. Your ma promised, and she wasn't a woman ever to go back on her word. She used to beg Mrs. O'Gorsebush, though, for leave to tell her husband. 'Husbands and wives ought not to keep secrets from each other,' she used to say. I've come to see she was right."

Louisa couldn't help it: tears were spilling over and running down her cheeks. Her mother and the brownie's wife, drinking coffee right here in this dugout. She swallowed hard.

"What happened next?" Jessamine pleaded. "Please!"

"Och, for a time things went on well enough. Especially after the bairn came—that's ye, child." He eyed Louisa with apparent hostility, as if her growing older were another impertinence in his view. "Och, but me missus was fond o' that bairn. Ye. I expect she'd ha' given yer ma leave, sooner or later, to tell ye about us. Else she'd have had to go back into hidin', wouldn't she, when ye grew into a spyin' little rapscallion like all the Big Folk's small fry!"

He humphed, startling the chicks, who had found a line of ants snaking across the dugout's dirt floor and were busily snapping them up with their tiny beaks. Louisa felt a powerful longing to run away somewhere and have a good cry. Her ma's loss had never struck her so deeply as it did now. It was as if she could see, in her mind's eye, the life she might have had if Ma had lived: learning to make tiny clothes for the brownies, sitting in the afternoon shade having a chat with the brownie's wife . . .

"But what happened to your wife?" asked Jessamine, growing impatient.

"Och, well. After the young mistress died—beggin' your pardon, lass," he added gruffly, "I don't mean to grieve you—the heart went right out o' me wife. She began to fade again, worse than before. By then, o' course, the young master had built the fine frame house, and this house was sittin' empty, gatherin' dust. Me wife used to come and sit inside, still and silent for hours at a stretch. And she lost all caution; yer pa must have walked right by her here a dozen times, in broad daylight. But he always kept his eyes straight in front o' him, he did, on this part o' the path. Happen the dugout reminded him too painful-like o' yer ma."

"Yes," murmured Louisa. "I used to ask if I could bring my doll here to play, and he never let me. He said he wasn't sure it was safe anymore, that the roof might cave in someday."

"Aye, well, he's got sense, he has," said the brownie. "Needed a powerful lot o' shorin' up, this place did, when I first came to fix it up for me wife."

"When was that?" asked Jessamine. "Was it a surprise?"

The brownie gave a bitter laugh. "Ye might say that. I worked and scraped for weeks on end, firmin' the walls, evictin' the rodents, sweepin' and shinin' and cuttin' shelves. And I went to no end o' trouble huntin' up nice things to cheer the place with. Almost broke me neck gettin' that fool dolly down off yer Missus Sour-Smirk's mantel."

"You mean Mrs. Smirch?" asked Louisa, clapping a hand to her mouth.

Jessamine giggled outright. "Mrs. Sour-Smirk. It fits her."

"My kind always know the true name o' things," said the brownie. "That woman's glare would curdle milk!"

Louisa turned away so he wouldn't see her smile. The brownie hardly seemed one to talk about *glares*.

"Well, in the end 'twas all for naught. I never got to show her the surprise. One mornin' I come home from a hard night's work over here—gettin' that fool oilcloth into place over the ceiling, and no easy time of it did I have, let me tell ye—and she bursts into tears at the sight o' me and says that's it, she's had enough, it's bad enough havin' lost the society of everyone else she ever cared for, now I'm out gallivantin' all night and sleepin' all day, and never a nice word do I have for her, and—" He was so worked up that he actually gave a little hop, frightening the chicks so thoroughly that they all poured out the open door at once. The brown hen clucked reproachfully over her shoulder as she hastened after them. "Gallivantin'! Me! I ask you."

He snorted in disgust.

"And so she left?" asked Louisa softly.

"That very morn. Half a year ago, 'twas. I've nae seen her since. I've asked every flyin' thing for ten miles round for word o' her, but the last anyone saw o' her, she was trippin' toward the Big Folks' town with a bundle on her back and her skirts tucked into her apron. Six months, and nary a word. Six months!"

And suddenly he grabbed the edge of his cap in both hands and yanked it down hard, so that it completely covered his face. He wheeled around, turning his back on the girls and making peculiar choking sounds inside his cap.

Is he crying? mouthed Jessamine, and Louisa nodded: *I think so.*

Suddenly she understood why he was so cross and hostile all the time. He'd been living with a knot of loss and fear inside him for all those months. She knew what that felt like. When she thought of Pa, it was like a stab to her heart.

Shyly, carefully, she laid her hand on the brownie's shoulder. He stiffened at once and his choking sounds ceased abruptly.

"I'm so sorry," she said. "You must miss her very much."

"Impertinence," came the gruff voice, muffled by the cap, but for once it didn't sound hostile.

CHAPTER TWENTY-ONE
Sudden Moves

SUDDENLY JESSAMINE GASPED. HER EYES WENT WIDE with horror.

"Louisa!" she cried. "I came all the way over here to tell you, and I forgot!"

"Tell me what?"

"The sheriff came to our house this morning! They found enough men for the jury. Your pa's trial starts tomorrow!"

"*What?*" Louisa felt drowned by panic. "Tomorrow? I have to go! I have to be there!"

She would have run out the door right that second, but the brownie took hold of her skirts.

"Now don't be hasty," he said, shoving his cap back

into place with his free hand. His eyes were bright and wet. He turned to Jessamine. "What exactly did the sheriff want with yer uncle?"

"He wanted him to come to town. They're all going, Uncle Malcolm and Aunt Mattie and the boys, they're packing up to leave right now. I'm to stay behind and see to the chores. The sheriff needs my uncle to bear witness at the trial. About the stolen goods he found in this dugout—" Her eyes went wide. "Oh! You can save your pa, Louisa! Just go tell them about the brownie, and how he was only borrowing things to cheer up his wife. I don't think they can send a brownie to jail, can they?" She wrinkled her nose doubtfully.

Louisa and the brownie looked at each other. For one flashing moment hope welled up inside her, but it ebbed away just as quickly. The brownie glowered at her with the same surly hostility as always, but she saw, now, that behind it was something else. He was terribly, terribly afraid.

"I can't tell about him," she said at last, turning to Jessamine. "They might not put him in jail, but they'd try to catch him for sure, and study him, and keep him for a pet, like as not. No." She shook her head. "It wouldn't be right. My mother wouldn't have done it."

The brownie gave her a long, sharp stare.

"Ye know," he said, his voice so gruff it was nearly a growl, "ye look just like her. The spittin' image."

Louisa smiled, but in her heart the fear was stabbing again. Winthrop's taunt came back to her: *Your pa's gonna hang.* . . . She couldn't save Pa by telling who the real thief was, but she couldn't let him be hanged, either. She tried to think of what she could do, but nothing came to mind. Nothing at all. Except to go and be with him, and to beg the judge to be merciful.

"I have to go to town," she said. "I have to see Pa."

"But you'll never get there in a day," Jessamine said. "Not on foot. Thirteen miles. It's too far."

Louisa swallowed back tears; she needed to be there. Suppose she was too late, and they convicted him? Sentenced him? Carried out the sentence?

Suppose she never saw him alive again?

It was not to be borne.

"I have to get there," she said. "I'll walk all night if I have t—"

"Pish, tosh, and horsefeathers," interrupted the brownie. "There's no need for ye to walk anywhere, goose. I've arranged a ride for ye. Ye'd ha' been on yer way half an hour ago if ye'd not tricked me into tellin' ye me life story. Impertinence. I'll see to it ye get there in time—*if* ye'll mind yer manners and speak softly.

And make no sudden movements," he added as an afterthought.

"A ride?" Louisa began, but before she could ask any questions, the brownie put his fingers in his mouth and whistled loud, sharp, and long. He stared out beyond Pa's fields into the southern prairie, squinting. Louisa stared too, and in a moment she saw a dark blur of movement, growing larger: something was rushing toward them, rapidly, in a gallop. A horse? A stab of thrilling joy went through her: had the brownie summoned a wild pony? There were herds of them out on the open prairie, Pa said. *I can't possibly,* Louisa thought. *Oh, how lovely, I'm going to!*

But the blur sped closer and it wasn't a pony at all. It was lean and bony, with coarse-looking brown-and-white fur and black horns curving up from a long, tapered head.

A pronghorn antelope?

"I'm going to ride a pronghorn?" she asked in disbelief.

The brownie stroked his beard and gave a satisfied chuckle. "Indeed ye are. It's a first in the history o' the world, I believe, so I hope it's grateful ye are."

"I . . . but . . . how . . . ," Louisa sputtered.

"It's the fastest thing I ever saw," breathed Jessamine. "You'll get to town in no time."

"But—"

"Whisht with your 'buts'!" scolded the brownie. "Hold still, now. Mind what I said about no sudden moves."

The pronghorn slowed as it entered the barnyard. Walking, it seemed a clumsy, ungainly thing, head bobbing low, giving little nervous snorts. It kept some distance between itself and the girls, its brown eyes rolling warily.

"'Tis good o' ye to come," said the brownie softly, very slowly spreading his hands wide in a welcoming sort of gesture. "The lass is aware of the immense honor."

Louisa wanted to nod, but she was afraid of startling the animal. The brownie's warnings had been so emphatic. She had the sense that the pronghorn might turn and bolt at the slightest provocation.

How on earth was she supposed to ride it?

"He can cover sixty miles in an hour, unencumbered," said the brownie. "He'll go slower with a great goose aboard. Mind ye hold on tight, now."

CHAPTER TWENTY-TWO
A First in the History
o' the World

ONCE, ON ONE OF THE FEW TRIPS TO FLETCHER
Louisa had ever made, she and Pa had stopped to watch
a train pulling out of the station. Louisa had never seen a
train before. It was bigger and longer than she had imagined possible: the great curving wall of locomotive, like a
house made of metal, and half a dozen more houses lined
up behind it. It had inched forward slowly at first, the
black steam billowing out of a fat stovepipe, slow, slow,
then faster, faster, picking up speed, whistle screaming,
then as fast as wild ponies, racing away from the town
at top speed.

That was what riding the pronghorn was like. The
brownie had directed her to place the milking stool

beside the animal's back—slowly, slowly!—to boost herself up. She slid her leg across its back, afraid to breathe, afraid of pulling its hair or hurting it with her knee, afraid of kicking over the stool or doing anything wrong that might startle it and crush her one chance to make it to town in time for Pa's trial.

Such slow, creeping work, getting herself astride the creature—and then *whoosh*! She was racing out of the barnyard like that train. Faster than the train. Bouncing, jangling—oh, it was terrible. Her teeth knocked against each other, and she couldn't catch her breath. The pronghorn's back was ridged with bony knobs. She would be black and blue before they got to the boundary of Pa's land—if she could even manage to hold on for that long.

Jessamine yelled something after her; she couldn't tell what. The pronghorn rolled its eyes back, peering at Louisa, but she was bouncing so hard, she couldn't focus. She felt herself sliding back toward its rump and clamped her legs together in panic. Suppose she flew right off the back end?

With her legs squeezing tight against the pronghorn's sides, riding was suddenly easier. The tighter she squeezed, the less she bounced. She hoped she wasn't squeezing *too* tight, but then it occurred to her that being squeezed was probably less annoying to the pronghorn than having something heavy bouncing on its back over and over. She leaned forward, holding tight to its muscular neck, feeling the coarse fur against her face. Her hair was everywhere, and so were her skirts. Flapping fabric could startle a horse, but there was no way she was letting go to tuck anything in.

The pronghorn seemed to know which way it was going. Louisa hoped it did; she certainly wasn't about to try to steer it. Across the ruffled prairie she could see the green ribbon of trees that marked the creekline all the way to Fletcher. If she'd been hiking on foot, she'd have cut to the creek first and followed its muddy path to town. But the pronghorn kept to the open plain, loping roughly parallel to the creek but not venturing near it. Perhaps the terrain was too rough there.

She had no sense of how rapidly they were traveling. Faster than she had ever moved before, even on a galloping horse, that was sure. The pronghorn moved so differently: the movement of its legs was at once stiff and smooth, like two sets of pendulums swinging together, then apart, in unison. Louisa stopped trying to think of what it was like and just let herself ride and *feel*. Two kinds of wind: hot prairie breeze and cool rush of air from the speed. Prickly fur. An earthy, rank smell, like Evangeline but weedier, greener. Sun on her arms, sun hot on her hair. An ache in her leg muscles. She was glad of the ache, the exertion required to keep her seat. It eased the knot inside her.

She wondered where the pronghorn would put her down. On the one hand, it would be rather exciting to be carried right into town this way—the only human ever to ride a pronghorn, the brownie had said! Imagine the look on Mrs. Smirch's face!

On the other hand, it was hard to imagine any creature as skittish as the brownie had cautioned her this one was, daring to trot boldly up the main street of a human township. She felt rather shy about doing such a thing herself, come to think of it. *I must be a sight,* she thought. *Hair like a tumbleweed, and streaks of dirt on my dress.* She began to hope fervently that the pronghorn would drop her on the edge of town, where she might at least wash her face in the creek and braid her hair before she entered the town in search of the courthouse.

In all the excitement of the brownie's tale and the pronghorn's arrival, she had clean forgotten to grab her bundle of clothes and food.

But it was still early in the day, and the sky was hot and clear. Perhaps, if she could get the pronghorn to stop on the outskirts of town, she could rinse out her dress in the creek and let it dry before nightfall. The trial wasn't

She leaned forward, holding tight to its muscular neck, feeling the coarse fur against her face.

to start until the morrow. There was time. Even if her clothes didn't dry all the way, a clean, damp dress would be better than a filthy, dry one.

Of course, figuring out a sensible plan was a far cry from communicating that plan to a wild animal, Louisa thought. She wished the brownie had come with her; his ability to converse with the pronghorn would have been worth putting up with his grousing and insults. And if only there were some way he could explain to the judge and the Smirches and everyone else about taking all those things and putting them in the dugout . . . but no. Louisa knew what she had told Jessamine was correct. The brownie would be in even greater danger than Pa was. Probably.

Your pa's gonna hang.

It couldn't be true, could it? Did they really hang people for stealing? Horse thieves, yes—she knew they were sent to the gallows. Stealing horses was a serious crime. But a doll, a clock, a hatchet? Were those thefts enough to land a death sentence? Not that Pa had stolen anything at all, but Louisa had to admit that, from the point of view of someone who didn't know anything about the brownie, the case against her father looked pretty grim.

The stabbing thoughts tumbled and churned inside

her. She had to save Pa. Had to. But it would be wrong, wouldn't it, to sacrifice the brownie's freedom in order to secure Pa's?

The brownie ought to make the sacrifice himself, she thought. That would be the right thing to do. But it was clear that wasn't going to happen. He wasn't a human; he didn't live by human laws. He didn't even seem to understand that what he'd done—stealing things from Louisa and the Smirches—was wrong. He seemed to feel entitled to help himself to payment for his services: looking after Pa's livestock, tending the Smirches' hazel grove.

Whatever happened to Pa, Louisa realized, the brownie's part in it was over. He would go on watching over the hens and the chicks, chatting with the owl, grumbling at the earthworms, no matter what fate met a couple of Big Folk who hadn't even known enough to leave out a dish of cream now and then.

It felt hopeless. *But I'm riding a pronghorn antelope,* Louisa told herself. *If that can happen, anything can.*

CHAPTER TWENTY-THREE
Three Miles from Town

THE EMPTINESS OF THE PRAIRIE BEGAN TO FILL UP, barns and sod houses rising up out of the blowing grass. The pronghorn was no longer paralleling the creek; it cantered a zigzag path, skirting homesteads and wagon tracks. Louisa would have lost all sense of which direction held home if not for the great blue range of mountains hunkered against the sky: she knew they marked west. Fletcher was west of home. All the farms meant they were drawing near to Fletcher. The closer you got to town, she knew, the thicker the neighbors.

She tried to flatten herself against the pronghorn's back so that no one would see her atop it. She supposed it was one reason to be thankful for the sad state of her dress: all that dirt would help her blend in, from a distance. Despite the entertaining notion of prancing into town on the back of a wild animal, she was afraid that a curious onlooker might cry out and alarm the pronghorn. She wouldn't like to be thrown off at this speed.

Anyway, the pronghorn seemed to share her desire to escape notice. Just when Louisa was beginning to think she could make out the humped shapes of buildings ahead, a cluster of buildings too many in number to be some fellow's farm, the pronghorn veered far to the south, keeping to uninhabited land. Louisa began to hope very hard that it would stop soon, or she might be forced to fall off on purpose. She couldn't afford to stop too far outside town, and there was still her dress to wash.

Suddenly the animal slowed to a walk. It was breathing hard; she supposed she was quite a burden for a beast unused to carrying anything heavier than the wind. It was approaching a copse of trees, and Louisa could see the jagged brown gash of a creek bank sliced into the scrubby plain. Was it Spitwhistle Creek, or some other waterway? Was this where she should get off?

The animal's sides heaved and quivered; Louisa realized it was trembling. It shook its head, snuffling, its eyes rolling white. It came to a stop. *Am I supposed to get off now?* Louisa wondered. Awkwardly she patted the pronghorn's neck. It kept rearing its head back. She decided it was telling her to dismount, so she swung her leg over its back and slithered downward, feeling for the ground with her toes.

As soon as she was planted on the ground, the pronghorn leaped away from her, turned tail, and ran. It was gone like a shot, its white rump patch the only thing left visible above the brown and gold grasses.

"Well!" said Louisa aloud, feeling a little put out. The ride itself had been a great kindness, she knew, but she had not expected to be dumped in the middle of—where was she, anyway?—all alone, with nothing to guide her but the mountains and her wits. And those last felt positively scrambled after the jolting ride.

She took a few halting steps toward the creek bank. Her legs felt weak and wobbly. She wondered how far a walk it would be into the heart of town from here. Surely the pronghorn wouldn't have left her worse off than when she'd started.

The first thing was to figure out where she was. The blue wall of mountains: west. Home was due east of town. The pronghorn had traveled west from her home, then veered to the left, south. That meant town was north, or northwest. If she put the mountains on her left . . .

There. A sprawl of buildings. A curve of some hard-packed track. A grain silo.

Town.

Pa always said distances could be misleading out here on the prairie, but as best she could judge, she was no more than a mile or two from the closest buildings. Perhaps three miles from the center of town. An hour's walk, no more. Plenty of time to wash her frock, let it dry a bit, and reach the jail by sundown. She was powerfully hungry, but there wasn't anything to be done about that. Fool that she was, she'd left home without so much as a hunk of cornbread.

CHAPTER TWENTY-FOUR
The Best Worst Day

LOUISA KNELT BY THE CREEK TO WASH HER HANDS and face. The windy ride had left her parched, and she was glad to slurp a drink of cool water out of her cupped hands. Then she looked around one last time to make sure she was really alone, here on the fringe of town. She would not like any strangers to see her in her shift while she was washing her dress.

Everything was still and quiet, but she had the eeriest sense that someone was watching her. The skin on the back of her neck prickled. She turned in every direction, squinting hard at the empty grassland, the curve of creek, the smudge of buildings that meant town. The few trees that marked the creekline were gaunt, twisted things, blown half-sideways by the endless prairie wind. They wouldn't provide cover even for a brownie.

Don't be a goose, she told herself sternly. There was no one there, nothing but fluting wind and crickets scraping and the whisper of the creek. The gold and brown grasses rippled like water, bright where the sun hit them and dully shadowed where clouds sailed overhead.

Then one of the shadows rose up and unfolded itself into a lean, shaggy shape on four skinny legs.

A wolf.

Its mouth was open, the wet teeth glinting. Its eyes stared right into hers. Louisa's fingers went cold. Far back in her mind, a little screaming rabbit voice was hollering *Run! Run!*, but she couldn't move. Her legs wouldn't move. It didn't matter anyway; the wolf was too close. She couldn't climb a tree this time. It could spring on her in half a second.

Another wolf rose to its feet beside the first. Then another. Another. Five of them, forming a half circle around her. Louisa's heart hammered. Perhaps they were behind her too, ringing her.

A crow cawed from somewhere nearby, and she wanted to shriek to it, to tell it to go tell the brownie to send help, but her voice wouldn't work. Nothing worked. She remembered how the pronghorn had been trembling when it let her off, how it had flashed away so quickly without so much as a glance in her direction. It must have scented the wolves and bolted for its life, never minding what the brownie had asked it to do.

All the wolves were looking at her. Was it always like this? she wondered. Did they always frighten their prey by staring it down?

The first wolf advanced toward her slowly, one step, two. It was still looking right into her eyes, its terrible muzzle parted into a ghastly wolf-smile. Well, she supposed it had a lot to smile about. She didn't even have hooves to score a blow or two with before they devoured her. It took another step closer.

And then the wolf did the strangest thing: it crouched low, its front legs outstretched, its rump high and the great sweeping tail wagging back and forth. The wolf shook its head playfully, its grin wider than ever. It was almost as if it were trying to make friends.

That isn't possible, thought Louisa. Wolves were the deadliest terror she could think of, next to wildfire—and wrongly accusing neighbors. Grown men were afraid to ride out anywhere alone without their guns. It was worse in winter, of course, when game was scarce and the wolves were starving, but Louisa knew darn well there was no good time to run into a wolf.

It was still looking right into her eyes,
its terrible muzzle parted into a ghastly wolf-smile.

Another wolf trotted forward from the ring, its tail wagging to beat the band. This one came right up to Louisa's feet, so close she could feel its breath on her bare legs, and dropped something out of its mouth into the grass.

Louisa looked down. It was a hazelnut.

"The brownie sent you!" she cried, and the wolves grinned as if they understood her words. Suddenly the whole pack was frisking around her—the five she'd counted and more besides; she'd guessed right about there being more wolves behind her. The first wolf nudged the hazelnut with his black nose, and she bent and picked it up. It was slimy with wolf-slobber, and she thought it was the nicest present anyone had ever given her.

"Thank you," she said to the wolf, and it grinned and nuzzled her hand. She found herself stroking its dusty, shaggy fur.

"I'm petting a wolf," she said out loud. *I met a brownie, I rode a pronghorn, and now I'm petting a wolf.*

If her pa weren't about to stand trial, this would have been, Louisa realized, the very best day of her entire life.

CHAPTER TWENTY-FIVE
Town Jail

SNUGGLED UNDER THE STARS IN THE MIDDLE OF the wolf pack, Louisa figured that she was probably the safest person for hundreds of miles around. She had washed her dress in the creek and dried it in the clean, grassy wind, and the wolves had shown her a thicket of blackberries on the far side of the creek. Berries didn't exactly fill your belly like a nice bit of bread and cheese, but they had been fat and sweet, and she had gobbled them by the dozen. When the evening chill set in, the wolves had pressed close around her, a kind of living blanket. In the dark their eyes were like the stars above her, points of light in the blackness. Their breath panted like whispers all around.

The wolves nuzzled her awake in the early dawn, when the sky was rose-colored cloth sprigged with gold. She brushed the wrinkles out of her dress as best she could, scrubbed her face well, and rebraided her hair into tight, neat plaits. The head wolf had let her hug him good-bye before she struck out toward the smudge of buildings that meant town, squeezing the gift hazelnut as tightly as ever Charlie had squeezed his beloved white stone.

She followed the dusty track until it turned into a hard-packed path. The smudge of buildings became a cluster of frame houses and shops. A child hauling water from a front-yard well eyed her curiously. She followed the wagon-rutted road to Fletcher's main street. Last night, she had worried that she wouldn't be able to find the town jail in time. Now she realized that she needn't have fretted: Fletcher wasn't big enough to hide anything. There was the school, the church, the saloon, the bank. The general store, where she'd gone with Pa twice a year since Ma died. And beside it, a small drab building she didn't remember ever having noticed before, marked JAIL.

Next to the jail, an even tinier building bore the label COURTHOUSE. A crow perched on the courthouse roof, surveying the street with a lordly air. It fixed Louisa with a glittering black stare, then lifted its broad wings and flapped across a dusty yard to the porch of a neighboring house. The busybody manner with which it craned its neck to peer in the window made Louisa smile; it looked for all the world like it was spying on someone inside.

But no crow, no matter how comical, could hold her attention for long. Pa was inside that jailhouse. Hesitantly, Louisa pushed open the rough door. The sheriff, a stocky man with mournful eyes, stood at a small tin stove in the front room, pouring himself a cup of coffee. He looked up at her in surprise.

"Why, you're Jack Brody's girl, aren't you?" he asked, setting down the coffeepot.

"Yes, sir."

"Matilda Smirch said you run off. Folks've been worried sick about you. Where've you been?" asked the sheriff. "I thought your pa was like to knock down the walls of this here jail, wanting to go hunt for you."

"Please," Louisa begged. "May I see him?"

The sheriff opened and closed his mouth, as if he'd been about to say something and thought better of it. Louisa wondered what kind of awful things Mrs. Smirch had told him about her.

"I'm right glad to see you safe and sound," said the sheriff at last. "It was resting heavy on my mind that I left you with . . . er, folks who . . . er, well." He looked embarrassed, his brow puckering as if he wished he'd kept his mouth shut after all. "C'mon, I'll take you to your pa."

Pa was sitting on a bare, skinny mattress in a small iron-barred cell. He sat stone-still, hands on his knees, until he heard the footsteps and looked up.

"Louisa!" he cried, leaping to his feet. "Darlin'!"

"Oh, Pa!"

She ran to the cell, reaching for him through the bars. The sheriff made gruff sounds and unlocked the door.

"I reckon you'd like a minute to catch up," he said, his eyes more mournful than ever. "I'll have to lock you in, I'm afraid."

"O' course," said Pa softly. "I appreciate it, Chester."

The key clicked in the lock, and the sheriff exited hastily to the front room.

"Oh, Pa," repeated Louisa, burying her face in his shirt. His arms were strong around her and his whiskers prickled the top of her hair.

"Pa, you have whiskers!" she said, drawing back in surprise.

"They don't allow razors in here," said Pa, his eyes crinkling at her the way they always did. How could he smile, even in jail? But then his eyes were full of tears and he hugged her, hard.

"Where've you been, Louisa? The sheriff came in

yesterday afternoon and told me you'd run away from the Smirches! I about went crazy, locked up in here knowing you were out there alone somewhere, with the wolves and who knows what!"

Louisa choked back a smile. If Pa only knew!

"I was all right. I'm sorry, Pa, I didn't mean to scare you. I just couldn't stay there anymore. Mrs. Smirch . . . she . . ." She trailed off, unsure how to explain without mentioning the *critters*, and then she'd have to explain how she happened to get rid of them.

Suddenly she realized that the brownie would just *have* to let her tell Pa about him. She couldn't keep a secret like this from Pa. But getting leave to tell, and telling, could wait until after the trial. Right now the important thing was to save Pa's neck—literally.

But Pa was still going on about her having been missing.

"Where'd you go, Lou?"

"I was hiding, Pa. Near the hazel grove. I was fine. Yesterday I went home to our place to get some fresh clothes, and Jessamine found me and told me about the trial, so I came here."

"You came all that way on foot in one day?" asked Pa. He pulled back to look her in the eye. "Louisa, how on earth—"

"I hate to bust in on you like this, Brody," interrupted the sheriff, clearing his throat, "but the judge just came out his front door. Means I'd best get you next door."

"That's fine, Chester," said Pa, his voice all quiet and calm once more. He tucked in his shirt and slicked his hair with his palms. Louisa wished the sheriff had let him shave; he looked so scruffy this way. She hoped the jury wouldn't be swayed by his appearance. He'd been doing chores when the sheriff rode up to arrest him that day, and here he was in the same worn work clothes, looking none too clean after a week of wear. *Never mind my dress,* thought Louisa. *I ought to have had the sense to bring him a change of clothes.*

Pa caught her anxious scrutiny and flashed her a sudden grin.

"Look a sight, don't I?" he said. "Like someone I wouldn't want to meet skulking around my property on a dark night."

"Oh, Pa!" cried Louisa.

"Don't you worry, honey. Maybe we'll get lucky and the jury'll be nearsighted, all twelve o' them."

But Louisa saw the grim look in his eyes behind the cheerful words. Pa, she realized, was scared.

CHAPTER TWENTY-SIX

The Truth, the Whole Truth, and Nothing but the Truth

"ALL RISE FOR THE RIGHT HONORABLE JUSTICE Cornelius P. Callahan!"

Judge Callahan took his seat and surveyed the crowd in the courtroom. "Courtroom" was perhaps too generous a term for the small, bare, sawdusty room the good citizens of Fletcher had provided for its legal proceedings, he reflected, but it was a sight better than some of the places in which he'd held trials. There was a hamlet in the southern tip of the county that had no more to offer him than a milking stool in someone's barn. Fletcher, as county seat, tried to do things up as properly as it could.

The tiny room was crowded with gawkers. The

judge was not surprised; the trial of an upstanding and well-respected farmer like Jack Brody for the dastardly crime of thievery of tools and personal objects was a matter custom-tailored to rile the interest of the Fletcher townfolk. There were the Smirches in the front row: the two towheaded boys, jumping and climbing all over the bench; Malcolm Smirch, looking miserable in his Sunday clothes; and that pinchmouthed wife of his, fairly quivering with excitement. Judge Callahan could swear he saw her lick her lips, like someone about to tuck into a feast.

The rest of the benches were stuffed with townfolk: women and youngsters, mostly, and on two front benches, the jury—an array of men demonstrating varying levels of reluctance and eagerness. It was always an interesting feat, the judge reflected, to scrounge up enough fellows for a jury in these frontier towns that it was his fate to serve. Most of the men the sheriff approached made excuses—some of them not wanting to sacrifice a day's work, and the rest not wanting to involve themselves in proceedings that might wind up arousing vengeful feelings in a convict's kin and known associates. Chester Morgan had done quite well, thought Judge Callahan. No luck procuring lawyers, though, it seemed. Well, so much the better. The less speechifying, the better, in the judge's experience.

The door opened and in came the sheriff, holding tightly to the upper arm of Jack Brody. Brody held his head high, his face calm and resolute. Behind them walked a young girl in a rather dingy dress, her hair tightly braided. Someone made room for her on the edge of a bench. Her eyes were huge pools of worry. Judge Callahan sighed. He could almost hear Mrs. Mack sniffing "Poor motherless lass" in her indignant way.

Why wasn't the girl up front with the Smirch couple? the judge wondered. Weren't they supposed to be looking after her? Well, he supposed if he were the Brody child, he'd want to keep his distance from his father's accusers as well.

Enough. The judge gave a sharp crack with his gavel on the table before him, as much to order his own thoughts as to quiet the folk in the courtroom. It was time to be impersonal, to hear the evidence and sift through the lies and misunderstandings to get at the truth. The truth was always there, like a nugget of gold in a prospector's pan, but you had to wash away all the dirt and creek slime and fool's gold before you could see it.

The Fletcher bailiff was old Amos Pinker, who spent most of his time playing corncob checkers on the porch of Jed Button's general store. He spruced up for his courthouse duties by washing the tobacco juice off his bare feet and combing a handful of lard into his hair. As his hair was decidedly sparse on top, his generous hand with the lard resulted in a shiny pate streaked with clumped strands that lay in greasy parallel formation from his wrinkled brow to the nape of his neck. Judge Callahan was fond of old Amos. He was fond of anyone who took his work seriously, and Amos—on those infrequent occasions when work actually confronted him—met it with a most serious vigor indeed.

"The court will hear the case of one John Warrington Brody, charged with the theft of personal property, namely one hatchet, one pocketwatch, one fine ticking clock in good working order, and one heirloom china doll most, er, beloved of its mistress." Old Amos shrugged doubtfully as he echoed the phrases he'd been given by Mrs. Smirch in the tense moments before the prisoner's arrival. Mrs. Smirch gave a sharp nod of satisfaction. Judge Callahan, watching the girl in the back of the room, saw how her lips tightened and her hands clenched white.

"We'll hear from the accuser first," said the judge, and Mr. Smirch came forward to take the witness's oath. Old Amos stepped forward with a Bible, and Mr. Smirch laid his left hand upon it.

"Raiseyerrighthand," intoned Old Amos. "Do you—er, what's your first name, son?"

"Malcolm," muttered Mr. Smirch.

"Do you, Malcolm Smirch, swear to tell the truth-thewholetruthandnothingbutthetruthsohelpyouGod?"

"I do."

Mr. Smirch took his spot on the tall stool in the witness box. Judge Callahan listened quietly as he recounted the events at Jack Brody's farm the week before. Smirch's story seemed straightforward enough. His hatchet hadn't been in its usual spot, so he'd walked to Brody's to borrow his; it appeared that Brody was quite neighborly in this regard, obligingly lending his tools or his time whenever Smirch needed assistance. While Brody was sharpening his own hatchet for Smirch's benefit, Smirch's boy had gotten into Brody's old dugout and found there the very hatchet Smirch had misplaced, along with his pocketwatch, his seven-day clock, and his wife's china-headed doll.

At the mention of the doll, Mrs. Smirch dabbed at her eyes with a handkerchief, but Judge Callahan couldn't for the life of him detect any trace of moisture in those hard, eager eyes.

"All right. So I'm given to understand that these objects went missing from your place, and they were discovered on the property of Mr. Brody here. Is that a correct assessment?"

"Yes sir, your honor."

"Other than the fact that the items were found on Brody's property, do you have any evidence that 'twas Brody himself who took them?"

"Well, no, your honor, but—"

"Fine, fine. And before this day, when you found your things in his dugout, how would you have characterized Mr. Brody?"

"Characterized, your honor?"

The judge noticed several members of the jury furrowing their brows. One of the perils of a classical education, he often reflected, was a predilection for vocabulary of an obfuscating nature. He tried afresh.

"What sort of man would you have said he was?"

Mr. Smirch frowned, crushing the hat he was holding. "Well, I dunno. I guess I'd have said he was all right. Uh, I mean, he's been a good neighbor to us over the years. Until this." His eyes darkened. "I thought he was my friend. Until he started stealin' things from right under my nose."

The gavel rapped down. "That's enough. We'll not go leaping to conclusions quite yet, sir. You may return to your seat."

Mr. Smirch stood, his hat completely crushed between his two large, calloused, angry hands. He strode back to his seat on the front bench, gesturing exasperatedly for his boys to slide over and make room for him again—their fidgety bodies had oozed sideways to fill all available space. Mrs. Smirch stood up and smoothed her bonnet strings, clearly expecting to be the next witness called. It was always amusing to Judge Callahan that the very folks who had least to do with a case thought themselves vital to its progress. Mrs. Smirch had already made it plain, in interviews with the sheriff, that she knew nothing whatsoever about how the missing objects got from her home to Brody's dugout. She hadn't even noticed the doll was missing until her husband came home with it.

"I'd like to hear from the defendant next," said the judge. Mrs. Smirch gave an offended sniff. A member of the jury chuckled—the town banker, the judge thought, or perhaps it was that fellow with the string tie who played piano in the saloon next door.

Jack Brody was sworn in and his story matched Smirch's, point for point. He hadn't been in the dugout for years, not since his wife died. They'd been in the frame house for several years before her death and the dugout wasn't used for regular storage.

"I don't reckon we've ever had so much to store,

your honor, that the barn couldn't be holdin' it," said the defendant wryly.

"How do you explain, then," asked the judge, "the appearance of Mr. Smirch's possessions in your dugout?"

"I can't explain it at all, your honor," said Brody. "I've been sittin' in that cell for a week, puzzlin' it out. I didn't put them there, and I know it wasn't my daughter. I asked her, and she always speaks the truth." He nodded at the child in the back of the courtroom, who sat tensely poised as if she might fly off her bench at any moment. She nodded back at her father, looking for all the world like a martyr about to be thrown to the lions.

"And you haven't seen anyone else on your property? No tramp or rover who might be using your dugout as a shelter?"

"No one, your honor. Since the last time I came to town—last April, it was—I've not laid eyes on anyone besides my own daughter and the Smirch family here."

"If it wasn't him, it had to be the girl!" cried Mrs. Smirch. "Impertinent thing, she is, and she's got—"

"Order, order!" shouted the judge, banging hard with his gavel. "Madam, you have not been given leave to speak in these proceedings. If your testimony is required, you will be properly sworn in before we'll hear one more word out of your mouth."

He beetled his brows at her, knowing from long experience how that cowed the most fiery-tempered heckler.

"All right, then, Mr. Brody. Before we move on, is there anything else you'd like to tell the court?"

The members of the jury leaned forward almost as one body, eager to hear what Brody had to say.

"Well, sir, only this: there were some o' my own things in that dugout too. Things I'd missed, and some I hadn't, but none o' them put there by me. Or by my Louisa. I don't know how they got there. And what puzzles me so, your honor, is that they weren't the sort o' things you'd expect a tramp to take. Say there was some poor feller without a roof over his head, and he happens along and sees I've got this old dugout sittin' empty. Why does he go and fill it up with a clock and a doll and a jar full of buttons? Wouldn't he be more like to steal food?"

Brody shook his head. "It just don't add up. We don't have much, your honor, but we've got a good amount of grub stored against the hard months. Salt pork, dried fish, berries, cheese, meal. Not a speck o' that has gone missin'. Come to that, all a fellow'd have to do is knock on the door and ask for a meal. But no one's done that, and no one's taken anything at all to fill a hungry belly, and the things he did take were set out in that dugout as pretty as you please. I have to say, your honor, I'm as eager to know the truth of the matter as you are."

Mrs. Smirch broke out into accusatory cries once more, and all over the courtroom was a gabble of whispers and speculations. Judge Callahan hammered on the bench until the ruckus died down and told Brody to return to his seat.

"We'll hear from your daughter next."

Privately, the judge had begun to work out an explanation that made sense. It contradicted a piece of Brody's testimony, but Jack Brody wouldn't be the first parent to have a blind spot where his child was concerned.

It had to be the girl.

The clock, the doll, the old dugout—it made sense. The child probably had fond memories of living there when her mother was alive. She'd decided to fix it up as a playhouse, and once she started, well, she must have gotten carried away.

Not that it was a light matter, oh no. It pained the judge to think of having to bring the child's actions to the scrutiny of the crowd in the courtroom. She'd done wrong, for certain. Not just taking things that didn't belong to her, but lying to her pa and letting him be carted off to jail . . .

Poor mite, she'd probably been living in fear and

misery all week. And yet, as he watched her walk bravely down the center of the room toward the dock, her small chin held high just like her pa, meeting his gaze directly, it gave him pause. Judge Callahan had seen many a guilty party in his day, and this child didn't behave like a person with a great weight on her conscience.

Ah, well, he'd have the truth out of her soon enough.

Old Amos stepped forward with the Bible. "Do you swear to tell the truththewholetruthandnothingbutthe- truthsohelpyouGod?"

The girl hesitated, one hand on the Bible, the other raised to take the oath . . . but she shook her head. Her hands dropped.

"I'm sorry." She looked at the judge, her eyes beseeching. "I can swear to tell the truth, and nothing but the truth—but I can't swear to tell the *whole* truth."

His Honor Cornelius P. Callahan had heard a good many startling pronouncements in his day, but this one, coming from this mite of a lass, took the prize. At her words the courtroom had erupted into exclamations, the voice of the agitated Mrs. Smirch rising above them all like a train whistle.

"You . . . what . . . I never . . . ," sputtered the judge. At last he collected himself and gaveled the chattering masses into silence.

"Would you mind explaining that remarkable statement, young lady?" he asked severely.

"Yes, sir," whispered the girl, cutting an anxious glance at her pa. He was staring back at her with the same anxious expression.

"I can tell you it wasn't my pa who took those things," said the girl. "Nor I. But . . . but . . . I can't tell you how they got into the dugout."

"You can't, can you?" The judge's voice was stern. "But you do *know* how they got there?"

"Yes, sir." The girl was looking him straight in the eye. He couldn't fathom it. She was admitting right out that she was hiding the truth, but she behaved with the calm conviction of a person who knows she has done nothing wrong.

The judge stared back at her, meeting her steady gaze. Then, suddenly, he banged his gavel on the table.

"This court is in recess," he boomed. "Child, I'd like a word with you in private."

CHAPTER TWENTY-SEVEN
Especially When It's Hard

THE FLETCHER COURTHOUSE WAS A ONE-ROOM affair, offering no such amenities as judge's chambers.

"We'll just step across the yard into my sitting room," Judge Callahan told Louisa.

She followed him quietly to a small two-story house beside the courthouse. A crow perched on the roof, eyeing them alertly. The judge clumped up the porch steps and stomped his feet hard before opening the door.

"Mud," he explained laconically. "Now, we'll just come right in here." He spoke loudly, causing Louisa to wonder if he were perhaps a little hard of hearing. "SIT RIGHT HERE, YOUNG LOUISA."

He settled himself into a chair opposite her and leaned forward, eyeing her intently.

"Now, I'd like to know what on earth you mean by refusing to take the oath in my courtroom. Do you know, lass, that in forty-two years of practicing law, I have never heard of a single instance when such a thing occurred? I've seen plenty of folks in a right hurry to take that oath and spew out half a dozen lies, but no one ever refuses to speak the oath itself!"

Louisa swallowed. She did not know how she could possibly make him understand without giving away the brownie's secret.

"I can swear to tell the truth," she began. "I will anyway, whether I swear it or not. My pa taught me to tell the truth always, even when it's hard. *Especially* when it's hard."

"And yet here you are, refusing to speak it."

"Not exactly, sir—your honor, I mean. I mean, I beg your pardon. Your honor."

The judge waved a hand impatiently. "Never you mind about the your-honor business. Speak plainly, child."

Louisa took a breath.

"I'll tell you the truth. I didn't put any of those things in the dugout and neither did my pa. That's the truth. And nothing but the truth."

"But . . . it isn't the whole truth?"

"No, sir."

Judge Callahan pursed his lips and stared off over her head with narrowed eyes and a creased brow.

"But don't you see, child, that I have to know the whole truth if I'm to help your pa?"

"Well, I was thinking about that, and I don't think you do," ventured Louisa.

"You don't!" the judge exclaimed, surprised. "Explain yourself!"

"I was thinking that even when people tell you everything they know—the whole truth—like my pa did, and Mr. Smirch, too, it doesn't mean all the answers are there. Sometimes there's a part of the truth that no one knows. Isn't there?"

"Hmm. I suppose there is. Go on."

"In this case, there's a part of the truth that I know, but I can't tell it without going back on a promise. And I mustn't do that, because that's a kind of oath just like the one I couldn't take."

"Child, if you're protecting someone . . . if you've made a promise under duress . . ."

"What's that?"

"It's when someone forces you to promise something against your will. With threats, or . . . or mistreatment of some sort."

"Oh," said Louisa. "No, it isn't anything like that. No duress."

The judge sighed. He was staring off past Louisa again, gazing intently at the mantelpiece above her head. *His eyebrows waggle up and down when he thinks,* Louisa observed.

"Is there nothing else you can tell me, child? Nothing at all to help clear your pa?" He looked at her shrewdly. "You're sure you didn't fix up the dugout yourself, as a kind of playhouse?"

"Oh, no!" cried Louisa. "I hadn't been inside it since before my mother died, when I was little. Until that day with Winthrop and Charlie, the Smirch boys. Mr. Smirch had come over to borrow my father's hatchet because he couldn't find his own. And then Winthrop got into the dugout—those boys get into everything—and he saw his father's hatchet right there beside the door, and came running back to the barn, shouting about it."

"And then what happened?"

"We all went up and looked inside, and Mr. Smirch came out with the clock and the doll."

"Did you go inside the dugout yourself?"

"Not then . . . later." Louisa's voice was soft. She was terribly afraid of slipping and giving the brownie away.

This judge seemed very smart. Surely he would see that Pa was innocent and there wasn't a case against him, wouldn't he? Even if he never got to the bottom of who the real thief was?

"Tell me what you saw inside the dugout, child. Your pa said it was fixed up 'pretty as you please.'"

"Yes, sir, that's right." She described the oilcloth, the shelves, the jar full of buttons, her mother's fine comb so carefully displayed.

"And you have no idea who arranged those things so nicely?"

Louisa clamped her mouth closed. She dared not say another word.

The judge sighed again and struck his thighs with his hands. "Blast it, child! There's something you aren't telling me! It's as if you're protecting someone . . . wait."

He leaned forward. "You have a friend."

Louisa held her breath.

"Someone you don't want to get in trouble."

Louisa couldn't help it: she looked away, afraid he would somehow read her thoughts through her eyes.

"Aha! I know! Haven't I heard that the Smirches took in a child? A niece, wasn't it? Lass about your age?"

Louisa quailed in alarm; it had never occurred to her Jessamine might be brought into this. But before she could utter a word, a shrill voice cut into the tense hush between Louisa and the judge.

"Cornelius P. Callahan, you old fool! Are ye not satisfied with browbeating one child—ye've got to falsely accuse another?"

"What—what—" choked the judge, rising to his feet. He appeared to be addressing the mantelpiece behind Louisa's head. "What are you thinking, madam? YOU'LL BE SEEN!"

Louisa whirled around. To her astonishment, there was someone standing on the mantel. A very small someone in a brown frock, with a tiny flowered apron tied around her ample waist—and a tall pointed brown cap upon her tiny head.

"What?" she gasped, hardly believing her eyes.

Judge Callahan sputtered. "Thunder and lightning, what more surprises can this day possibly bring?"

He stepped forward, putting a hand on Louisa's shoulder. "Child, allow me introduce you to my housekeeper, Mrs. Angus MacClellan Brody Callahan O'Gorsebush."

The brownie woman held out her hand.

"How d'ye do, Louisa dear. You may call me Mrs. Mack."

"Thunder and lightning, what more surprises can this day possibly bring?"

CHAPTER TWENTY-EIGHT
Potato Chowder

LOUISA GAPED.

"You're the brownie's wife!"

"So ye *have* met my husband," said Mrs. Mack. "I thought as much." She looked at the judge. "That's who she's protectin' here, the lamb. My fool of a spouse."

"I'd no idea you had one," said the judge weakly. He flopped back into his chair.

"He misses you," said Louisa shyly, feeling an urgency to convey that important fact to the brownie's wife. After all, he had done so much to help her, no matter how grumpily. "He was fixing up the dugout for you. That's how all this started."

Mrs. Mack snorted. "Misses my fine cooking, I suppose."

"No, ma'am, it's more than that," insisted Louisa. "He was sad that you were lonely. He said so. He was fixing up the dugout so you could be close to me, I think. Like you were close to my mother."

Mrs. Mack gave her a penetrating stare. The judge started to exclaim over the revelation that Mrs. Mack had known Louisa's mother, but the brownie waved him silent.

"What else did he say?" she asked at last.

"That's what he was doing all those nights when you thought he was out gallivanting."

Mrs. Mack emitted a kind of squeak and hastened to the far end of the mantel, twisting her apron furiously. Louisa and the judge exchanged embarrassed glances.

"I, er, thought it was the niece," said the judge. "The little girl who lives with the Smirches. Fixing up the dugout as a playhouse."

"Jessamine," said Louisa. "No. But she's the one who saw the brownie first. I'd never have known about him if it weren't for her."

Mrs. Mack came striding back down the mantel, her eyes suspiciously red.

"Well," she said. "Well. This is all very interesting, it is."

"He's worried about you," said Louisa. "And he has your things just like you left them. Your chair, with the pine-needle knitting needles. You make the loveliest knitted lace," she added.

"He showed you our home?" asked Mrs. Mack, astonished.

"He let me stay the night," said Louisa. "When I ran away from the Smirches. It was very kind of him." Mrs. Mack was staring at her with such astonishment that Louisa felt uncomfortable. "And he got a pronghorn antelope to bring me to town, so I'd be here in time," she added, babbling a little to fill the silence because Mrs. Mack was looking at her so strangely.

Now it was the judge's turn to cry out in astonishment. "You rode an antelope?!"

"Yes, sir. They're very fast."

The judge snorted. "'They're very fast,' she says, as if she's passing the time of day. Child, you astound me."

"I was kind of astounded myself."

"I shouldn't wonder."

"Well," repeated Mrs. Mack. Her voice was bright and brisk, bearing no hint of the emotion that had been welling out of her eyes a moment before. "Well! This is all very interesting, and it melts my heart to see you again, lass, grown so big and looking like yer bonny ma. But we ought not to be standing here jabbering while yer poor pa's over there worrying himself sick. The first thing to do is to get this child a bite to eat. Fair starved to death, she is, or I'm no judge!"

She clambered down from the mantle by way of a conveniently placed hat rack. As Louisa followed Mrs. Mack to the kitchen, the judge bringing up the rear, she realized that the whole house was laid out with such conveniences in mind. A cunning arrangement of stools and flour barrels made it possible for Mrs. Mack to climb from floor to table with ease. A cracker barrel stood next to the iron stove, its flat top at the perfect level for the brownie's wife to stand on while stirring the big iron pot that simmered on a back burner.

The judge pulled out a chair at the table for Louisa and pushed it in behind her, just as if she were a grand lady. She smiled up at him in thanks. He gave her a solemn wink in reply.

"How long have you lived here, Mrs. Mack?" Louisa asked timidly. There was something about the tart briskness of the brownie's wife that was even more intimidating than the brownie's surly insults.

"Nigh on six months," replied Mrs. Mack. "Came by

crow, I did. I'd not seen this town since that first time yer folks came through, afore ye was born—and then only what I could spy from our hiding place in their wagon."

She ladled some kind of thick, fragrant broth from the big pot into two tin mugs. The judge carried them to the table and set one before Louisa.

"Here you go, lass," he said. "There's not a finer potato chowder in all the world."

Louisa's stomach was so empty she could almost have made a meal on the chowder's aroma alone. It smelled delectable, but remembering the brownie's terrible tea, she raised a small and tentative spoonful to her lips. At the first taste she nearly swooned. It was the most delicious stew she had ever eaten, rich and buttery with a whisper of nutmeg.

Mrs. Mack beamed approvingly. "I'm glad to see ye've an appetite."

"It's the best thing I ever tasted in my life," Louisa said between bites.

"Didn't I tell you?" said the judge.

"Pair of fools!" clucked Mrs. Mack, obviously pleased.

Gradually, over the mugs of soup, the judge and the brownie's wife unfolded the tale of how Mrs. Mack had come to be his housekeeper. At first Mrs. Mack had found the house empty—"empty of Big Folk, that is, but crammed with his books and triptraps"—because the judge had been out on the circuit, visiting the other towns he served. Mrs. Mack had enjoyed "queening it up," as she said, in a house all by herself, with high ceilings and a proper kitchen. But it was lonely. And loneliness, Louisa gathered, was what had driven her to leave the brownie and their home under the hazelnut trees in the first place.

"Then, one day, in clumps this great noisy brute of a man, tracking mud on my nice clean floors," said Mrs. Mack.

"*Your* floors?" said the judge, arching an eyebrow. Mrs. Mack ignored him.

"Och! I hastened into hiding but 'twas clear to him someone had been in his house while he was away. He searched the place, but I stayed out o' sight." She sighed. "After that, for a while, things was like they used to be in the Auld Country. He lived here, and I helped out in wee small ways, but 'twas frankly unsatisfying for both of us. What use had I for his silly dishes o' cream, I ask ye?"

"You knew, then?" Louisa asked Judge Callahan. "That you had a brownie? And you knew what to do?"

The judge nodded.

"Aye. I grew up in the Auld Country myself, didn't I?"

"How did you finally happen to meet?" Louisa asked.

"It was my doing," said Mrs. Mack. The judge grinned. "One day I just grew weary o' always having to scuttle about, sewing on his loose buttons without being caught, choking down his god-awful bowls o' porridge . . ."

"*You* cooked for *her*?" asked Louisa, giggling. It was comical to think of the judge making porridge for someone who could cook as marvelously as Mrs. Mack.

"Aye," said Mrs. Mack. "And one day I couldn't bear to think o' choking down another bite. So I crept in here early one morning and made a nice mess o' grits and eggs, and fresh blackberry muffins. I laid it out on the table all nice and hid over there behind the teakettle to watch him. He walks in, he does, and takes a good long sniff, and he says—"

"I said, 'Begging your pardon, madam, what took you so long?'"

Louisa burst out laughing. Chuckling, the judge scraped up a last spoonful of stew and swallowed it with a satisfied sigh. "Delicious as ever, Mrs. Mack. But I ought to be getting back. They'll be wondering what has happened to us."

"Aye, Cornelius," said Mrs. Mack. "You go back over

there and settle matters with yer courthouse tomfoolery. I'll look after the lass."

The judge nodded and rose from the table. "Take your time, Louisa. It'll take us a while to round the jury back up. I shouldn't wonder if half of them have gone home for dinner."

He paused at the door. "I ought to retire after this case," he added. "I'll never have one to top it."

Louisa watched him go, gulping down the last of her soup. The burst of merriment was gone; she was thinking about Pa again. She was no longer worried that he would hang, but it struck her that even if Judge Callahan found a way to settle the trial without convicting Pa, people would always suspect him. His reputation would never be the same.

"What ails you, child?" asked Mrs. Mack.

"People think my pa's a thief," she poured out. "They'll go on thinking it always, even if the judge doesn't convict him."

"Perhaps. And that husband o' mine doesn't seem inclined to do anything about it."

"Well, he helped me get here for the trial," said Louisa.

Mrs. Mack snorted. "I'm afraid that wouldn't have helped overmuch if the judge hadn't already been acquainted with me."

"That's true," said Louisa.

"My husband," said Mrs. Mack. "Always so cautious. Hidebound, that's what he is. This is a new country, that's what I told him when I met your ma. A new country with new ways o' doing things. Why should we creep around a farm in secret, way out here in the middle o' nowhere, where neighbors are scarcer than hen's teeth? I like a nice chat over a cup o' tea now and then, I do! But there, lass, how I do go on. Och, look at you. You're pale as flour."

"People will *always* think Pa's a thief. Mrs. Smirch will never let it go." Louisa sighed miserably. "I bet she'll never let Jessamine visit me again either. I'm a thief's daughter, as far as she's concerned."

Glumly she stood and began to help clear the dishes off the table. She found Mrs. Mack's dishpan and placed the tin mugs inside with the soup ladle.

Suddenly she had an idea.

"Mrs. Mack," she gasped. "I know how to clear my father's name. If only—how fast do you think a bird can fly?"

Chapter Twenty-Nine
Elflocks

As the judge had suspected, most of the jury had taken advantage of the recess to slip home for dinner. It took over an hour to round them back up again and settle the noisy crowd. The courthouse was fuller than ever.

Jack Brody was scanning the room in visible alarm, obviously wondering what had become of his daughter.

"Don't you fret over your lass," said the judge amiably as he took his seat behind the table. "She was in sore need of a good meal. She's over at my place now, tucking into a dish of the best potato chowder this side of the Atlantic."

He picked up his gavel and paused, savoring the

last moments of calm before the ruckus he was about to cause. All eyes were upon him. Mrs. Smirch leaned forward hungrily, eager to see justice served upon the man who had by all accounts been as fine a neighbor as any homesteader could wish. Judge Callahan shook his head. Forty-two years on the bench, peering into the truth, and people were still a mystery to him. What curious satisfaction would it give this Smirch woman to see her neighbor packed off to prison in Topeka, or worse? Was her soul so shriveled that she didn't blink an eye at the thought of orphaning a child?

Thinks she wants justice, she does, thought Judge Callahan. *Lord help her if she ever gets it.*

He banged the gavel down. The faces of the jury registered impatience, eagerness, boredom. Many of the onlookers had drifted away during the long recess, perhaps having their own rumbling bellies to attend to.

"Upon reflection, it is this court's opinion that there is not sufficient evidence for a case against Jack Brody. I'm dismissing the charges."

The room exploded with noise. Mrs. Smirch's outraged screech rose above the din. The judge pounded and pounded for order, but it was several minutes before anyone took heed.

During this commotion, Jack Brody and the sheriff sat quietly side by side, both evidently stunned by this abrupt conclusion to the matter. The judge noticed the courtroom door opening and Louisa creeping in, struggling to lug the judge's old carpetbag that he used on his circuit rides. Judge Callahan's eyebrows rose. He had a strong suspicion that his housekeeper was hiding in that carpetbag. *She couldn't stand to stay home and miss the excitement*, thought the judge. *Ah, well, who can blame her?*

Quietly Louisa shoved the bag under a back bench. Then she sought out her father, squeezing her way through the crowd toward him. At the sight of her, Jack Brody rose to his feet with a glad cry and wrapped her in a bear hug.

Mr. Smirch stood watching, his nervous hands crushing his hat into a shapeless ball of felt; but Judge Callahan could swear that the man's expression was actually one of relief.

Regrets starting this ball rolling in the first place, he does, thought the judge.

But his wife was still shrieking for justice. "He's guilty, I say!" Mrs. Smirch screeched, eyes bulging, spittle flying. "It's a crime to let him go free!"

"Hush, Matilda," said Mr. Smirch.

"But he took our things!"

"No, madam," said the judge. "You discovered your things in an abandoned building on his property—"

"*I* discovered them," boasted Winthrop. The judge silenced him with a fierce glare.

"As I was saying, there is no evidence that Jack Brody took them."

"It's the same thing! Who put 'em there, if he didn't?"

Judge Callahan sighed. This could go on all day. This Smirch woman was clearly not the sort to let a grievance go easily. Most likely she would pester both himself and Jack Brody about this matter until the end of their days. The judge envisioned a well-deserved retirement marred by venomous missives, by passionate upbraidings whenever Mrs. Smirch happened to pass him in the street. He supposed it would be even worse for Brody, living a scant two miles from the Smirches. And the poor lasses, Louisa and the Smirch niece—what was her name? Jessamine—living away out in the lonely country, needing each other for company. With Mrs. Smirch harboring such a grudge against the Brody family, the girls would never be allowed a friendship. *'Tis a crying shame*, thought the judge. *If only there were some way to persuade her to let the matter drop.*

But her angry gesticulations made it clear she

would never let the matter drop. Now the sheriff, her husband, and three members of the jury were having to forcibly restrain her from clawing Jack Brody's eyes out.

That was when the judge noticed something peculiar. Swinging from Mrs. Smirch's bonnet string was a large round ring of keys. As the judge watched, the woman jerked away from her husband's grasp, causing the key ring to fly up and whack her in the cheek.

"Oof!" she grunted. "Who hit me? Someone hit me!" She whipped her head around to survey her restrainers, and the keys swung out again. This time they smacked the sheriff in the nose.

"OUCH!" he roared. "Have you gone mad, woman?"

"I didn't lay a hand on you!"

"I think you did, Mattie," said her husband warily. "Look, his nose is bleedin'."

Mrs. Smirch whirled to look, and the keys swung out again, striking her husband on the ear.

"Owww!" he yelped. "Mattie! What in tarnation have you got tied to your bonnet string?"

Mrs. Smirch started to whirl toward him, causing the entire jury to drop to the ground, avoiding whatever strange weapon the woman had tied to her bonnet strings. Judge Callahan sat watching in bewildered amusement.

Of the crowd around Mrs. Smirch, only Jack Brody hadn't ducked. He put out a hand and caught the swinging key ring, stilling it as calmly as one stopping the pendulum of a clock.

"Sheriff, these are *your* keys, if I'm not mistaken."

Mrs. Smirch cried out in surprise. "What? But . . . how . . . I've never seen these keys before in my life!"

A glimmer of understanding came to the judge. Could it be? He scanned the courtroom, searching . . . Surely Mrs. Mack would not be so foolhardy as that. It would be madness to risk exposing herself to the citizens of Fletcher. But someone had tied those keys to Mrs. Smirch's bonnet, and it was clear the woman herself had known nothing about it until they smacked her in the face.

Ah. Judge Callahan began to see.

"Madam," he said, his strong voice cutting above the din, "this is a grave matter indeed. Stealing from the sheriff—"

"But I haven't stolen anything!" cried Mrs. Smirch. "I have no idea how they got here!"

"And yet," said the judge, "there they are. Stolen property, on your person."

He paused a moment to let the statement sink in. The piano player began to chuckle.

"Oh, Mattie," said Mr. Smirch. He seemed deadly serious, and Judge Callahan had to look very hard to see the hint of a twinkle deep down in his eyes.

"Ain't that a puzzler," said Jack Brody.

"*You* done it—" Mrs. Smirch began, but she was shouted down by the crowd.

"Brody didn't do nothin'," growled the sheriff. "I've been watchin' him the whole time. Or are you aimin' to accuse *me* next?"

"Well, well, well," said Judge Callahan, enjoying himself mightily. "It seems we have another mystery on our hands. You say you didn't take those keys, Mrs. Smirch. And yet there they are, in your possession. I must say it doesn't look good for you, madam."

"But your honor," faltered Mrs. Smirch. She groped for Winthrop's head and clutched him by the hair. "Please. I'm innocent. My babies—"

"Ow!" hollered Winthrop, ducking away from the swinging key ring.

"As I said, it doesn't look good for you. And yet . . ." The judge paused, waiting for Mrs. Smirch to look him in the eye. "Perhaps you'll agree that despite the way things *look*, we have no real evidence against you."

Mrs. Smirch bit her lip.

"Perhaps you'll agree that sometimes, there are not

enough facts present upon which to form a sound conclusion."

"Well, I . . ."

"I thought as much. In that case, Sheriff, if you are content to retrieve your misplaced property, we can let the matter rest."

The sheriff wiped blood from his nose and gave Mrs. Smirch a long, appraising stare. She began hurriedly untangling the knotted bonnet strings to free the key ring.

"I'm sorry . . . they're so tight . . ."

"Elflocks, my grandmother used to call them," said Jack Brody thoughtfully.

"What's that?" asked Mr. Smirch.

"Knots in things. String, or horses' tails, or what have you. Elflocks. When I was a boy, my granny told me about the wee folk—how you had to be kind to them, or they'd tangle your ropes and curdle your milk."

From the corner of the courtroom came a low, satisfied chuckle. It wasn't the piano player this time; of that, Judge Callahan was certain. He saw that Mr. Smirch, too, had turned and was peering hard in the direction of the gruff and throaty laugh.

The crowd began to squeeze itself out of the stuffy courtroom, spilling into the street. The Smirch boys tagged after the sheriff, evidently enthralled by the gory sight of his red and dripping nose. Mrs. Smirch hustled after them, shaken, holding a hand to her bruised cheek.

Louisa launched herself at her father. Brody put his arms around the girl and held her tight. The two of them looked as if they could go on hugging all day; Judge Callahan was surprised when the girl pulled away and said, "I'll be back in a minute, Pa," and dashed out the door into the mobbed street.

Now Jack Brody, Malcolm Smirch, and Judge Callahan were the only three men left in the courthouse. The judge hung back, hoping for a moment alone with Brody, but Smirch stood frozen, rubbing his eyes.

"Something ailin' you, Malcolm?" asked Jack Brody kindly.

"No, er . . . ," replied Smirch, shaking his head as if rousing from a dream. "It's just . . . it's the darnedest thing. For a minute there I could have sworn I saw a— ah, never mind."

He shrugged, embarrassed. The judge saw how a fresh wave of color rushed over the man's face as he realized to whom he was making his strange confession.

"Jack," said Mr. Smirch weakly, "I . . . I don't know how to . . ."

"Don't mention it," replied Jack Brody. He put out a hand, offering to shake.

The two neighbors left the courthouse together in search of their children. Judge Callahan stood in the doorway, watching them go, feeling a vast contentment. Then he slowly closed the door and held out a hand to the figure hiding in the shadows behind it.

"You'll be Mr. O'Gorsebush," said the judge. "A very great pleasure it is to meet you."

There came a squeak from under the back bench, and Mrs. Mack burst out of the carpetbag with her hands on her hips.

"Angus O'Gorsebush! Whatever are ye doing here?"

The little bearded man stepped forward and straightened his tall, pointed cap, which had been knocked askew when he ducked behind the door, dodging Mr. Smirch's gaze.

"Had to make sure things came out all right for the lass's pa, didn't I? I was aimin' to march right in here and tell Hizzoner the whole story, until I saw he'd already got matters well in hand." He turned to the judge and bowed with immense dignity. "I hope ye don't mind me interference with Mrs. Sour-Smirk there at the end, sir."

"I've seldom enjoyed myself more," said the judge.

"Angus." Mrs. Mack's eyes were full of tears. "D'ye

mean to say ye'd have let Big Folk see you—on purpose—
to save that man?"

"Aye," said the brownie. "What d'ye take me for,
woman? A boggart?"

"Oh, Angus," said Mrs. Mack tenderly, and now her
eyes were shining.

The judge saw that the brownie fellow's eyes, too,
were suspiciously wet. He turned away to give them their
privacy, but they were too busy hugging to notice.

CHAPTER THIRTY
A Hair Bow
Ain't a Hatchet

LOUISA HURRIED OUTSIDE IN SEARCH OF MRS. Smirch and the boys, hoping her plan had worked. There were any number of things that could go wrong. Suppose the crow didn't make it there and back in time, or suppose he went to the wrong house? Although he seemed like a most intelligent creature. Mrs. Mack had explained the situation to him while Louisa wrote a hasty note to Jessamine. She just wished Jessamine could be here for the fun.

We'll have all sorts of fun together if this works, she thought. *Mrs. Smirch just* has *to let her visit me, after all she's put us through.*

Mrs. Smirch was standing in the middle of a crowd

in the dusty street, venting her wrath to anyone who would listen, while the sheriff's wife picked at the knotted bonnet string, trying to free the ring of keys. The sheriff stood nearby, tipping his head back and pinching his nose to stop the bleeding and fussing at Winthrop and Charlie to stand back and let him breathe.

"I don't care what anyone says," declared Mrs. Smirch. "I know what I know."

"But, Matilda," said the minister's wife, "that's just it. You don't know anything."

"Maybe it's ghosts!" suggested the saloon's piano player. "I can't think of no other way them keys got tied to your bonnet. Maybe it's ghosts playin' tricks on the lot of you."

"There's no such thing as ghosts!" scolded the minister's wife.

A heated debate commenced. It seemed the entire population of Fletcher had an opinion about the existence, or lack thereof, of ghosts, and whether or not a ghost might—if one existed—be responsible for hiding assorted objects in Jack Brody's dugout and knotting the sheriff's key ring into Matilda Smirch's bonnet string.

Louisa stood in the thick of it, scanning the sky for . . . There. A dark dot, a smudge, moving fast across the blue. Mrs. Mack said a crow could fly twenty-five miles in an hour, and this one had flown twenty-six. *No, wait,* Louisa thought, *it's thirteen miles to the Smirch place by foot, but it must be a good bit less than that as the crow flies.* In any case, the crow had done it. Its strong wings beat steadily as it soared into town, dragging a little under the weight of the thing it carried in its talons.

Louisa wanted to cheer. How Jessamine must have laughed when she read the note!

"What in tarnation?" said the sheriff, squinting into the sky. "What's that fool bird carryin'?"

The townsfolk followed his gaze.

"It's just a stick," ventured the piano player.

"Naw, look at it," insisted the sheriff. "It's . . . it's . . ."

The crow swooped low and let the object fall from its grasp. It hit Mrs. Smirch right on the top of her head.

"It's Ma's ladle!" hollered Winthrop.

"What?" screeched Mrs. Smirch, clutching her head.

"Matilda!" called Mr. Smirch, pushing through the crowd. "What on earth?"

Winthrop picked it up. "It is! It's Ma's ladle from home!" He turned it this way and that, eyeing the dents. "I'd know it anywhere," he muttered. Charlie backed away from the ladle like he suspected it might jump up and crack him on the head too.

The crow swooped low and let the object fall from its grasp.

Louisa shot a glance at the crow, who had perched atop the courthouse and was watching the proceedings with a wide, laughing beak. She made a stern face, trying to telegraph a message with her eyes: *I said to drop it at her feet. I wouldn't wish a head smack from that thing on anybody.*

The crow cocked its head at her and spread its wings wide. It gave a lazy flap and lifted itself off the roof, swooping once more over the crowded street before lighting out for the open prairie.

"Well, I'll be," said Malcolm Smirch, watching it go.

"I never saw the like," said the minister's wife. "Maybe that's what stole those things from you folks." She fixed the piano player with a stern glare. "It most certainly wasn't a ghost."

"How could a crow carry a hatchet?" scoffed the piano player.

"Oh, you'd be surprised," chimed in old Amos, the bailiff. "My mother says that back in the Old Country, they had magpies that would steal a hair bow right off your head."

"A hair bow ain't a hatchet," said the piano player disgustedly.

"My grandmother used to say that in the Old Country, they had eagles so strong, they could cart away a full-grown sheep!" said the minister's wife.

"A sheep ain't a hatchet neither!" shouted the piano player, but it wasn't clear anymore what point he was arguing. Now half the town was chiming in with stories they'd heard from their mothers and grandmothers and hoary old great-uncles, tales of all the things the birds and beasts of the Old Country had spirited away from right under people's noses. Louisa couldn't help but grin. Her heart felt as free and soaring as the crow.

They won't blame Pa now. His name is clear.

Pa came up behind her and put a hand on her shoulder. The judge was beside him, carrying his carpet-bag. Louisa couldn't help but notice it was unfastened at the top. She glanced down, peeking inside, and two pairs of glittering eyes looked back at her. They were most certainly not badgers' eyes.

Very slowly, one of the eyes winked.

CHAPTER THIRTY-ONE

Top o' the Mornin'

AN EARLY OCTOBER SNOW DUSTED THE STUBBLY fields, and the nights had grown cold enough to warrant three quilts on Louisa's bed, but the afternoon sun shone brightly, pouring itself through the open doorway of the old dugout. Mrs. O'Gorsebush liked to watch the clouds move over the fields while she drank her tea. Proper tea, it was, not her husband's nasty horseradish brew. Mr. and Mrs. O'Gorsebush had brought a little sack of tea with them when they returned to the country after spending the past few weeks in town at Judge Callahan's house.

"Ah," said Mrs. O'Gorsebush, taking a deep, contented sniff of the steam coming off her eggcup teacup. "Does a body good, that does."

Louisa smiled, watching Jessamine gleefully spoon sugar into her cup—another treat Mrs. O'Gorsebush had packed into her bundle for the crowback trip from town. The judge (who, try as he might, could not get out of the habit of calling his housekeeper "Mrs. Mack") had just departed for one last circuit ride before winter descended, and the brownies had returned to their cozy home under the hazel grove.

"Och, 'tis grand to be back," said Mrs. O'Gorsebush. "I missed my nice teacups, and my knitting-wool. But it was right lovely in town as well, these past weeks. Angus and I are thinking of wintering with the judge. Waste away to skin and bone, he will, if I'm not there to cook for him." She took a sip of tea. "And Angus would sooner cut off his beard than admit it, but he was happy as a pig in muck puttering around that drafty old house, patching this and mending that. It's a wonder he didn't drive us all deaf with the hammering."

She leaned toward the girls, her eyes twinkling. "Don't you tell him I said so, but he's been practicing at tiddlywinks. He's determined to beat the judge when next they meet."

The girls laughed. Louisa felt a soaring happiness through her whole being—something like the way it had felt to fly across the prairie on the pronghorn's back. The brownies had been back in the country for a week, and already Mrs. O'Gorsebush and the girls had met for tea three times: once in the tunnel-house; once in Louisa's house; and this time, just for fun, in the dear old dugout that had, in a way, been responsible for bringing them all together. Louisa had swept it out, and Pa had carried down a little round table and three kitchen chairs for the occasion. Mrs. O'Gorsebush had pressed him to join them, but he begged off, explaining that her husband had offered to help him repair a hole in the barn roof. Evangeline was getting quite cross about it, the brownie had said—she didn't like the moon looking in on her at night—and Pa didn't want to vex her further.

It was strange to see Pa conversing with the brownies as casually as if they were any old neighbors. At first he had been dumbfounded by the full tale of Louisa's adventures after his arrest, but by the end of her account he was nodding thoughtfully, as if he'd done a tricky sum and the math had come out right.

"That explains a good deal," he had said, looking off into the distance—seeing, Louisa supposed, a long succession of small mysteries that made sense now, once one got past the shock of the brownies' existence. All those years, when she and Pa had thought themselves alone, they had really been helped by the keen attentions of their small neighbors.

"I've never lost a single animal to illness or accident," Pa had said. "That's quite remarkable, when you think about it. I wonder I never thought about it! I suppose . . . I suppose I only noticed what I *did* lose."

"Ma," said Louisa.

"Yep. Mrs. O'Gorsebush tells me her heart near broke into pieces when your mother died. She said she always regretted makin' your ma promise not to tell me. Said she'd have let her out of the promise soon enough, if she'd lived."

Louisa had been thinking about her mother's promise and how that secrecy had taken things in one direction when the whole truth might have taken them in another. Not that Ma might not have died—not even the brownies could cure every sickness—but she and Pa could have been friends with their unusual neighbors all along, helping the brownies as much as they themselves had been helped, and enjoying one another's company, and Mrs. O'Gorsebush would not have grown so lonely, she almost faded away.

And Mr. O'Gorsebush, too. Louisa understood now that his gruffness was a kind of protective skin he'd grown during those long, brokenhearted months after his wife disappeared. He was still gruff, but Louisa noticed he was spending an awful lot of time at the homestead ever since the brownies' return from town. Every morning when she went out to hunt for eggs, there he'd be in the barnyard with a full basket in his hand.

"Beat ye again, ye sluggard," he'd say. If Louisa invited him in for a cup of horseradish tea, he never turned her down.

In the dugout, Mrs. O'Gorsebush produced a basket of dried-berry scones and served one to each of the girls. Jessamine tucked in eagerly, and Mrs. O'Gorsebush clucked with satisfaction.

"We'll put some roses in your cheeks yet, lass," she said. "And Louisa, you're growing so tall, you'll have to let your skirts down soon!"

"Pa brought me six yards of calico when we sold the harvest," Louisa said. "I'll be sewing all winter, I expect."

"I aim to make Cornelius a new suit o' clothes while we're in town. It's a disgrace, a man o' his years and stature traipsing about with patched pants."

"You will come back in the spring, won't you?" asked Jessamine anxiously.

"Och, aye, to be sure, we will. We've got to keep an eye on ye, haven't we?"

Her tone was light, but Louisa knew that beneath

the mirthful retort, Mrs. O'Gorsebush was dead serious. She had taken an interest in Jessamine after hearing her history from Louisa, and she was determined to make sure that Mrs. Smirch treated the child kindly.

"But how?" Louisa had asked.

"I put it to her straight!" Mrs. O'Gorsebush had replied.

"You spoke to her?"

"That I did, and high time. Marched right into her bedroom as she slept, three nights ago, it was. I climbed on her pillow and shook her awake. She nearly died o' fright when she saw me." The brownie wife had laughed at the memory. "I told her straight out that I had my eye on her, and if she treated that little girl with anything less than a mother's kindness, I'd curdle her cream, tie knots in all her thread . . . and *put out the word to every louse in the county to pay a visit to her head!*"

The echo of those words made Louisa chuckle over her teacup. It was clear they'd made an impact: Jessamine's hair was neatly brushed and tied with ribbon, her dress was clean and patched, and she had been allowed to come visit Louisa every day. Louisa was teaching her to write, and Mrs. O'Gorsebush had promised to show them both the secret of her famous potato chowder.

"What are you laughing about, Louisa?" Jessamine asked, wiping scone crumbs onto a napkin.

"I'm just happy, I guess," said Louisa. "It's nice to have neighbors." She walked to the door of the dugout and looked at the sunlit path leading to the frame house and the barn, where Pa knelt on the roof beside the brownie, hammering a shingle into place. In the other direction the path ducked around a curve, and all she could see were those billowing fields, snow-speckled, thick with secrets. As she watched, the meadowlark rose up from the prairie, arching its way to the top of the barn roof. The brownie spit something into his hand—nails, perhaps—and commenced scolding the lark for disturbing him at his work. The lark tilted its head and trilled, sounding so uncannily like the brownie—*grumble grumble grumble*—that Louisa burst out laughing again.

"Now he'll scold it for impersonating a mockingbird," Mrs. O'Gorsebush said with a chuckle as she joined Louisa at the door. "Hullo! Who's that?"

Someone had just come around the curve of the path and was heading directly toward the dugout. Jessamine ran to look too, squeezing beside Louisa.

"It's a . . . what *is* it?" she said.

"It's a coyote," said Louisa uncertainly. "With . . . with two heads?"

"With two heads, and one of them's wearing a green hat!" put in Jessamine.

"No," said Mrs. O'Gorsebush, stepping right out of the dugout onto the path and waving her napkin at the visitors. "'Tis a coyote . . . with a rider. Well, my gracious. That's a leprechaun, it is, if I am not mistaken. Welcome!" she cried, sounding girlish and merry. To the girls she added, "Och, I've not seen a leprechaun in a donkey's age. Fine, merry folk, they are!"

The leprechaun lifted his green bowler hat and grinned a wide, toothy grin. His hair was as red as Pa's. "Top o' the mornin' to ye," he called. "Me name is Bobbin O'Brien, and this here's me good friend, Trickster. We've heard tell there be fine opportunities fer our sort out this way, and we've come to make yer acquaintance."

Louisa and Jessamine looked at each other. Jessamine's eyes were sparkling. *Pa's right,* Louisa thought. *This land is full of possibilities.*

She smiled and stepped forward to shake the leprechaun's hand.

"Might I offer you a dish of cream?"

"We've heard tell there be fine opportunities fer our sort out this way, and we've come to make yer acquaintance."

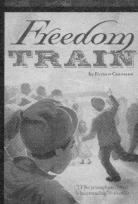